The Terrible Quin

John Brindley

Also by John Brindley

Amy Peppercorn: Starry-Eyed and Screaming

“Sixteen year old Amy Peppercorn has a lot to scream about. She's struggling with her A-levels and coping with her two year old sisters while her parents tear each other apart. Her best friend is being lured away from her. Then Amy falls under the spell of cool, elusive Ben and joins his band.
Winning Ben's approval means careering through the streets in a stolen car, skipping school, and staying out late. Amy could be in trouble. But she leaves the band behind - she's not like the others. She's going to be a pop sensation.
At the end of a stunning novel that packs a huge emotional punch, she is on the brink of stardom - but knows there will be a terrible price to pay.
John Brindley is a compelling and very distinctive writer with terrific insight into teenage relationships, hopes and fears. He writes brilliantly about the music world and the dangerous world of joyriding and police chases. This is a must-read.” READINGS.COM.AU

"This is a true delight of a book! Ideal for all ages and particularly suited to teenagers. Once you pick it up you will not put it down until you are at the last page!" ONLINEPOP NEWS

"A must read for anyone who wants to be famous." MIZZ MAGAZINE

For Danielle and Robert

THE TERRIBLE QUIN

This book crackles with a latent violence that is both gripping and stomach-churning. The children's betrayal by their uncle is as horrifying as it is believable. The reader becomes as protective of little James as Maria is, and as helpless in the face of the apparently psychopathic albino thug, the Terrible Quin. With only pages to go, my heart was in my mouth. Cliff-hanging stuff indeed.

Janni Howler,
TIMES EDUCATIONAL SUPPLIMENT.

One

Father

She storms up, Maria, slamming into her bedroom. That brother of hers – cruising for a slap he was, the little snot-rag. It was Dad this, Dad that - look, Dad, look what Maria's gone and done! That little sneak, telling on her the whole day. As if things weren't bad enough what with school and everything, boys, all of that, without a little brother like James always on your back, running to the old man, crying.

Like tonight:

'You little brat – you baby!'

'Don't say that to me!'

'Brat – baby!'

'Don't you say it!'

'Brat – little baby boy!'

'I'm telling Dad!'

'You're such a wimp, do you know that?'

'I'm telling Dad – Dad!'

'Wimp! Crappy little brat!'

'Get off me!'

'Shut up, you.'

'Dad!'

'Wimp! Want that, brat?'

'Dad! She's hit me! Maria's hit me!'

Typical, that was. The old man comes flying in, like he does, coming down hard on Maria as usual. It's always Maria, always. As if she didn't have enough problems to deal with, what with that Sandra at school. She was going to get it too, one of these days, that Sandra. Do you know what she said about Maria the other day, to Janet Brown and all that lot? Do you know what she said? Maria was livid. Sandra, she only went and told Janet Brown and her crew that Maria's mother didn't want Maria and James after her separation from their father. She told everyone Maria and James had to stay with their father because their mother wasn't having anything to do with them. That malicious lump, that greasy-haired, cheap nobody Sandra Pearce. What it was, was Sandra being jealous of Maria because that new boy Grant liked Maria better than her. But Sandra knew the truth, really. She knew that they had to stay with their father because their mother was always on the road with the Theatre. Sandra knew it, that lump of lard, but she always wanted to find a way of using information against you.

It wasn't the separation, or the divorce. Divorce wasn't anything. Nearly everyone's parents were the same, even Sandra's. Separated. Divorced. But Sandra was with her mum. Her mum! What a woman. No wonder Sandra was like she was. Sandra's mum, some flat-chested rake in an all-day shiny and slippery tracksuit, forever coming round the house, Maria's house, trying to do things for Maria's father. It made you sick. You only had to listen to her with him, with Maria's dad. They only lived down the road, Sandra and her skinny, slippery mum, so there was nothing to stop the tracksuit imposing, always appearing, supposedly wanting to help the poor man out. That poor man – that was what Maria overheard Sandra's mother saying to Sandra one day – that poor man, left on his own to bring up two children, and Maria so difficult as well.

So difficult! Maria would show then what difficult was.

Like now, storming up to her room feeling like getting her own back for once. Just for once, to be able to get one over on someone, to feel she had at least a little bit of power and control over her own life.

She turns on her music from the PC, speakers, not headphones for a change, giving it a good blast of the old volume. Dance music is hammering it out, the deep down bass thumping against the floor like a stampede. Maria's just getting into it when another stampede comes crazy up the stairs and crashes into the door of her room.

'Maria!' her dad's bellowing, snorting outside. 'Maria, turn that noise down! Now! Do you hear me? Maria?'

He's knocking hard on the door as the bass-bound music is booming across the floor, pounding into the cavity of Maria's chest.

'Open this door, Maria! Now!'

In the end, the old man wins. He has to, because he's been known to nearly throw a fit, with all his blood vessels sticking out like blue worms writhing down his neck. So he appears now, looking really gruesome as Maria opens the door and in he bursts, shouting down Maria and her dance music and the walls and the windows while he's at it.

‘Turn that row off! Now!’

So Maria switches it down and there’s this second’s silence before the old man’s high-horse gallops out and he leaps on it.

‘What’s the matter with you?’ he’s blaring, turning ever redder. ‘For Pity sake, why don’t you try to have a little thought for other people for once? Eh? Well? Say something!’

Maria shrugs. There’s nothing to say. When he’s like this, what can you say? You’re always in the wrong, so what’s the point?

But the old man, he can’t see it. He’s too busy being mad and wanting everything his own way to see that Maria’s saying everything there is to be said about it by saying nothing. He’s too involved with his own frustration with things he can’t do anything about, other than go all crimson, to realise Maria’s just as mad but reacting in a different way. The difference between them is that Maria knows when there’s nothing she can do about it all, so that’s when she chooses to do nothing. Her father, stamping and shouting, he expects Maria to do the same back at him, so he can really go into one. But she doesn’t do it, so he goes into one about that. See, either way, Maria’s on to a loser. Especially when that worm of a brother appears behind their dad making faces only Maria can see. Her father doesn’t know he’s there, because he’s too busy losing it. But he loses it even more when Maria finally gets fed up with that boy making faces and she goes for him. The old man goes for her and it all ends up in a big door-slamming session, everyone confined to his or her own room.

Maria gets herself ready for bed. School again in the morning. Winter, this is, freezing outside. Dark in the evening, school in the morning, nearly the whole week yet to come, this being only Monday. Tuesday tomorrow. Computer Studies, Maths, PE, English. What a day! School! Getting worse and worse every week. It never used to be this bad. Not bad at all, in actual fact. Maria used to do quite well. That was before, of course. Before Sandra had so much over her, when things still seemed okay at home. Sandra was a friend then, just a mate. They had played together after school nearly every day. Good friends they were, most of the time. But Sandra kept getting jealous. She was greedy – lumpy, jealous and greedy. Maria forgave her then, but not now. Not now she realised all Sandra needed over was a couple of nasty things and Maria's life could be hell. Sandra had that way of turning everyone against you so you felt on your own. You felt sometimes like slapping someone right in the eye, they were all so – so ...

She shrugs, shivers, trying not to get so knotted tight about everything, all that being on your own kind of stuff. It was all rubbish anyway, school, GCSEs, all of it. It doesn't mean a thing. If you were any good at any of it you'd only ever end up like her father, some kind of washed-up computer consultant with a failed marriage, struggling to make ends meet by writing for magazines and websites all about computers, while making such a bad job of bringing up two children whose mother didn't want to know them. Some prospect!

But then, there was the new boy, Grant. He was all right. He was brainy, you know, clever without being too intellectual, but he was cool. He was good at everything, you could tell by the way he didn't have to try at anything. He was just easy with things. Good looking, too. And he was seen to be on Maria's side the other day in another argument, she couldn't remember what it was about. It didn't matter. The point was, that Grant had been smiling at Maria for everyone to see, right when Sandra had been doing her best to wind Maria up again and set everyone against her. It was like a dream, being smiled at, just then, by Grant. It was the best thing that had happened to Maria for ages.

Still getting herself ready for bed, Maria's thinking about Grant so that she won't have to think about all the bad things to do with school. Like games, for instance. PE. Some schools, they didn't have to do it. Not theirs. All that prancing about. It didn't do anybody any good. If you were good at sports, you were good. If you weren't, you weren't. That was it. There wasn't anything any teacher was going to do that was going to make Maria suddenly start enjoying flouncing about on the netball court in a too-short skirt with Jimmy Bains and Johnnie Harris and their spotty greasy crowd smirking round the edges. It just wasn't right. Nothing was going to make Maria change her mind about that. And maths. English. Geography. Computer studies. What a bore! There wasn't ever anything real about it. It missed the point, totally.

So Maria's finally ready for bed, trying not to think about the craters round Jimmy Bains's mouth, or the little, horribly nasty comments Sandra kept making about her. Sandra! Always whispering, pointing Maria out to someone or the other, but then talking just loud enough so Maria could hear they were discussing her. Maria has to concentrate as hard as she can on the new boy Grant to prevent her mind being drawn back to Sandra and Jimmy Bains and netball and maths and the whole stinking lot of it.

But how can you concentrate at all when your nine-year-old brother's knocking on the wall between your bedrooms? That wall's nothing but a piece of board really, so the noise is like a hammering. Maria hammers back against the wall, knock for knock. The two of them end up smashing away at each other until their father's door opens, crashes closed.

'You can both stop that now!' he bellows from the landing. 'You hear me, you two? I've got work to do.'

With that, he stomps downstairs, and starts bashing away at the keys of his laptop. He hits it too hard, he's in such a strop. Maria lies awake listening to him as he attempts to batter his way through to the end of another article. Sometimes, at times like this, Maria can feel quite sorry for him. But she doesn't like to feel sorry for anybody, so turns over quick and settles for sleep.

But that tapping from downstairs is getting on her nerves. She can hear it too clearly, even through her doze. It brings her round, once, twice, three times. On the third time though, the phone's going, which stops the tapping.

Maria's nearly asleep. She can hear a voice, maybe Dad on the phone, maybe someone else. She goes off, dreaming about something breaking somewhere. The smash of it in her dream nearly wakes her again. But all's quiet. Sleep doesn't let go of her brain now. It wraps around it tight, holding her down deep until the morning comes and it's suddenly light.

Funny that, it being this bright first thing on a Tuesday morning in the middle of winter. Usually you had to get up in the dark for school, but not this morning. It was fully light and very quiet.

Then it wasn't so quiet, because Maria could hear the TV or the radio turning on. That was something that didn't usually happen in their house of a weekday morning, unless it was the holidays. There wasn't usually enough time.

Maria lay there for a while, listening, waiting for the knock on her door from her father. She waited until it felt all wrong, lounging in bed like this. Besides, you can only lie there so long before you've got to get up and go to the loo.

Downstairs, James has this natural history programme on about some kind of bird or the other. Maria's fed up to the back teeth of natural history programmes, especially those about birds – which is most of them. Did they always have to bang on and on about the same old stuff they've been on about for years? Every single bird was supposed to be in danger of extinction, or so they always said on TV. If you were to ask Maria, she'd tell you she doesn't believe any of it. Birds were everywhere. It didn't take a genius to realise that the programme was supposed to be more important if the bird was getting rare. Birds were boring, nearly all of them the same.

'Turn that off,' she tells James.

He just ignores her, like he does. He's so annoying. What could you do with someone who made out you didn't even exist, other than give them a knock on the top of the head?

'Ow!' he cries, over-exaggerating. 'I'm telling Dad!'

'I'm telling Dad!' Maria mimics his whiny little voice.

'Get lost, M'ria,' he says.

'What time is it?' she asks.

'I dunno.'

'You don't know anything, do you.'

'Get lost!'

So Maria, bored with annoying her brother, saunters out into the kitchen to get some cereal and have look at the clock. But she comes straight back in again, her face changed.

'Do you know what time it is?' She's serious, this time of asking, and worried.

'Get lost, M'ria,' James tells her, without looking away from the screen.

'No, James – it's nearly ten o'clock.'

'So what?'

'So what? It's nearly ten o'clock, that's what's so what. Are you stupid or something?'

'Get lost, dog-breath.'

'And you get a life, you thick-head. It's Tuesday morning. School started over an hour ago.'

James looks at his sister now. 'Did it? Where's Dad?'

Maria turns as she's going out. 'That's what I'd like to know.'

Going up the stairs, she's thinking how he never, ever oversleeps. He's mad on school and hates it when they miss a single day.

Downstairs, James switches channels on the TV using the remote. He's bored with the birds on the wildlife programmes. On the other side, some show for really little kids, you know the type, adults putting on stupid voices, talking to glove puppets, people dressed up to look like toys. It's so bad. But James watches it anyway, because even that's better than seagulls' nests and eggs.

He switches it back quickly as Maria's footsteps are heard galloping down the stairs. She bursts into the room as if to catch James watching the tiny tots' TV.

'Have you even seen Dad this morning?' She has this weird expression on her face.

'What you on about?'

'What do you think I'm on about? Have you seen Dad this morning, or not?'

'Not.'

Then she dashes out like a lunatic, dives back in. 'Are you mucking about?'

'How do you mean?' James asks her.

'Are you mucking about with me, James? Because if you are – '

'I'm not – I'm not! I haven't seen him.'

Maria stands there staring at him for a few more moments. 'Then he's gone,' she says.

Two

Mrs Pearce

'Get lost, M'ria,' James says again.

'I'm telling you,' Maria glares at him, 'Dad's not here. His bed's made. Some of his clothes are missing.'

'Where's he gone?'

Maria has to look away for a good few moments, sighing. 'What do you mean, where has he gone? I don't know, do I! If I did, I'd hardly be bothering to ask you – '

'Dad!' James calls out. 'Dad!'

'Oh!' exclaims Maria. 'Oh, yes, that's it – let's both stand here shouting Dad at the top of our voices, shall we? That's bound to do the trick.'

'Dad!' James calls again, as if Maria had been serious in what she was saying to him.

'Oh, be quiet, James, will you?'

'But where's he gone?'

'I don't know I said.'

'But he must be somewhere.'

'Yes, he must be somewhere, but he isn't here, is he, so there's no use your shouting the house down after him. His bed's made – maybe it hasn't been slept in. Maybe he went away last night because we were giving him such a hard time – you cry, James, and I'll whack you one.'

'I'm not crying.'

'No, but you look as though you might. Just don't, that's all.'

'Get lost, M'ria.'

'Yeah, okay. Then there'll be no one here but you. You'd like that, wouldn't you? Get yourself some breakfast.'

'I've had some. Chocolate biscuits.'

'Then you'd better go and clean your teeth.'

'I don't have to. I don't have to do anything you say, you can't make me.'

'James, just go and do it,' she tells him as she switches off the TV.

'I was watching that!'

'Oh, you are – you're such a pain, do you know that?'

'So are you!'

'I could so easily just kill all the little brothers in the world,' Maria is saying as she goes into the kitchen. But she stops, still and silent, as she sees a face peering in through the back window. Some face it is, too – thin, sloping, sly and slippery, with its eyes sliding this way and that. A hand taps against the glass.

Maria sighs. Oh no, Sandra hag-bag Pearce's mum, doing the rounds. Forever popping in there she is, thin as a coat-hanger holding up a tracksuit, the baggy leggings she wears appear empty, there's so very little leg in them. Maria has often wondered how they'd managed to get big-baby Sandra out of that rake. Mrs Pearce pregnant must have looked like a knot in a piece of wet string.

Mrs Pearce taps more urgently on the window. She was expecting Maria's father, not Maria. You can see by her thin but tense nostrils how she's already prickling with curiosity. There's nothing Maria can do but unlock and open the back door for her.

'Hello, Mrs Pearce.'

'Hello, Maria. No school today?'

'No.'

'You're not ill, are you, dear?'

'No, I – that is, I'm not ill as such. I'm just not quite well enough to go to school today.'

'Oh? What's the matter with you, then?'

'Oh – nothing, much. I'm just feeling too – '

'Who are you talking to, M'ria?' James wants to know, sauntering into the kitchen in his pants and tee-shirt.

Mrs Pearce looks at him, then at Maria again. 'James not feeling too good either, is he?'

'I'm all right,' James tells her. 'It's Dad,' he says, straight away.

'Your dad? What's the matter with your dad, Maria?'

'Nothing,' says Maria.

But, 'He's gone,' chips in the big-mouth boy.

'Gone? Gone where?'

'Just out – ' Maria attempts to say.

'We don't know,' the big mouth rattles, 'he's just gone. Vanished.'

'Vanished?' Mrs skinny Pearce barges her way past Maria. 'In what way vanished?' Her curiosity's fully up now. She's gazing round like a big-eyed broomstick.

'Gone,' James tells her, 'just like that.'

'His bed doesn't look as if it's been slept in,' Maria has to tell the woman, giving in. 'I've looked all over. He does seem to have vanished.'

'Vanished!' skinny, skanky Pearce is whispering, as if she's just witnessed an alien abduction. 'Vanished!' Whispering it again and again, her big eyeballs popping. Then she says, 'Have you checked in the loo?'

'Oh,' Maria snaps, 'do you know, I didn't think of that, Mrs Pearce. Did you hear that, James? Mrs Pearce thinks we should have a look in the loo.'

'Is he in there, then?' James asks, as Mrs Pearce exits, giving Maria a filthy glance before she goes.

'Of course he isn't in there,' Maria goes at her brother. 'Do you really think I'm so stupid as to not have had a look in there?'

'Then why did you say that to Mrs Pearce?'

'Go and get some brain, will you, James? You're so thick.'

'I'm not thick. You're thick.'

'Compared to you, I'm genius.'

'Compared to you,' James replies, straight off, 'everyone's a genius.'

'Do you know,' Maria has to admit to him, 'that's the first half-witty thing I've ever heard you say.'

'Yeah,' James nods, well pleased with himself.

They go into the other room while Mrs Pearce is to be heard banging about upstairs looking in all the cupboards. Maria and James don't say anything, but wait for the string-bean to appear again, still whispering. 'Do you know, you're right. He doesn't appear to be here.'

‘Oh, doesn’t he?’ Maria asks her. ‘Well, well, well!’

Mrs Pearce, who doesn’t like Maria at the best of times, looks down the bony ridge of her nose. ‘I have to check, Maria,’ she says. ‘So try to keep a civil tongue in your head, will you? I know it’s difficult for you, but do try.’

‘Why don’t you try minding your own business for once?’ Maria asks.

She nearly jumps out of the sag of her leggings. ‘Oh! Oh, that’s nice. And what would happen to you if I did? You can cope, can you, Maria? On your own, with little James to look after?’

‘I’m not little,’ James pipes up.

‘I can cope with this,’ Maria says, picking up the telephone receiver. She gives Mrs Pearce one shrivelling little smile before tapping out the emergency number, ignoring the disapproval in that woman’s stare.

‘Hello?’ Maria says, speaking slowly and deliberately. ‘Yes. I’d like the police, please. Yes, it’s an emergency.’

Then she gives the Pearce another piercing little grin. The tracksuit shifts and shimmers. Maria has a few words with someone from the emergency police services who tells her that a missing person, even a father of two, is not actually considered an emergency. Mrs Pearce gives out a tiny smile of her own as Maria has to take another number to call. But Maria calls it, coolly. It’s her local police station. Mrs Pearce just stands there with that same smirk on her face as Maria gives the details of her father’s disappearance.

'They're sending someone over,' Maria tells her as she hangs up. She wishes the woman would take the hint that she isn't needed, and certainly isn't wanted there.

'So,' Mrs Pearce tries to conclude, 'we've sorted that, at least. I'll make some tea, shall I?'

'There's no need.'

'No, I'd like to. Wouldn't you like a cup of tea, James?'

'Can I have chocolate?'

'Of course you can.'

Maria's left glaring at her brother as Mrs Pearce bustles off into the kitchen as if she alone belongs there.

'What?' James asks. 'What?'

Maria turns away from him in disgust.

They wait for the police to arrive. It takes a horribly long time. Much longer than any of them had expected. Maria and James get dressed. The tea and chocolate Mrs Pearce makes and then re-makes, gets cool, is drunk, the cups go cold, get washed up by Mrs Pearce. James gets bored out of his skull, has a kick around with one of the cushions, pretending it's a football, which he's not supposed to do. He thinks he can do everything he's not supposed to, because his father's not there to stop him. In the end, Maria has to have a go at him because of the fact that he's really, really getting on her nerves. He, naturally, isn't taking any of that from his sister, so bad-mouths her, which gets a reaction from her and they're off into a row. That only concludes when Mrs Pearce steps in out of the kitchen to calm them both down but gets told by them both (but mainly by Maria) to kindly mind her own business.

The three of them end up annoyed and frustrated, waiting in stubborn silence for the law to get there at long last.

When they do finally arrive, they come in, a man and a woman, both in uniform, asking all the same questions as Mrs Pearce, making the same dumb assumptions, that Maria and James are just stupid kids without a clue. Well, James is, as far as Maria's concerned, but she most definitely is not. She interrupts when the policeman or woman start asking Mrs Pearce questions, just to let them know that that woman knows nothing about it, or any of them.

'When was the last time you actually saw your father?' the policewoman asks her.

'Last night, when I went to bed.'

'And how was he?'

'How was he?'

'Was he – happy?'

'Happy?'

'No,' James opens his big mouth, 'no, he was cross. Really bad.'

'Really bad?' asks the big male copper. 'What, cross about something in particular, or just – '

'Just cross with us,' says Maria, 'with me and big-mouth there. We were fighting.'

'She was starting on me,' James tells the man, as if he might get him to arrest his sister.

'How cross was he?' the policeman wants to know. 'Worse than normal?'

'Normal?' interrupts the streak in the baggy tracksuit.

Both the police officers look at her, but say nothing. She says nothing more, for the moment.

'Was he,' puts in the policewoman now, 'more upset than he'd normally get at you two for fighting?'

'Yes,' blurts James.

'No!' – from Maria, straight away. 'I mean, he wasn't so upset. Not so upset as all that.'

At that, they're all sitting there looking at Maria, with the police people trying to weigh up the situation.

'I tell you what,' suggests the policewoman, 'would you and James mind going upstairs for a little while, so we can have a proper word with Mrs Pearce here?'

Straight off, James is up and on his way out. Maria stands there. She has bad feelings about leaving Mrs Pearce here to speak on her behalf. 'I'd rather stay,' she tells them. 'I'd like to hear what Mrs Pearce has to say.'

At which James halts, turns back.

'Please, Maria,' the woman says, taking Maria by the arm, turning her towards the door. 'I'm sorry to have to ask this of you, but it is necessary.'

'Why?'

'Come on, M'ria,' James says, opening the door.

'We'll call you when we want you to come back down.'

Maria shrugs the hand from her arm. 'I'm going,' she says as she shoves past James. He follows her out into the hall and up the stairs. But halfway up, Maria turns. James nearly clumps into her.

'Where are you – ' he starts to say.

She quietens him. 'Follow me,' she whispers, slipping back downstairs to where the door's left slightly ajar. She and James crowd at the opening, listening hard.

They hear Mrs Pearce, saying, 'It's difficult to say, really. He's ever such a nice man, but under so much pressure. From that girl especially.'

'You old bat,' Maria whispers.

'How well do you know him, Mrs Pearce?' the policeman is heard to ask.

'Ah, well now – we're friends, you know?'

'No,' answers the man, 'we don't know.'

'Well, we are friends, neighbours, helping each other. He – I don't know – he's a man. But I've never encouraged that in our relationship.'

'Oh, sure,' whispers Maria.

'We share a common need. Simple companionship. I wouldn't want anything to spoil that.'

'But you do know him well enough to gauge his moods?' the woman asks her.

'Yes – yes, I expect I do.'

'And has he been – upset, lately?'

'No more than usual.'

'And what's usual?'

'You have a guess. You've talked to the girl.'

'Rotten old bat,' Maria whispers, hoarsely.

'So he can be pretty moody? He can get upset can he, being in the house the whole time?'

'We all can. But he's a man. It's worse for a man, I always think.'

'And what's the outcome? Severe depression?'

'Sometimes.'

'Sometimes?'

'Yes.'

'Like now?'

'Yes, like now.'

'And do you think this severe depression could lead to drastic acts? Acts of violence, do you think? Or despair?'

There's a long silence. Maria's whispering throughout it, going, 'No, no, it's not that bad. She doesn't know. She's just a nosy old bag. She doesn't know a thing.'

But then Mrs Pearce decides to answer, with, 'Yes, I expect it could lead to – '

And before James knows what's going on, the door's shoved open by Maria and she's back in the room amongst them, going, 'No! She doesn't know! She doesn't know anything! It isn't like that! She doesn't know a thing!'

But James has moved to the other side of the room because he's spotted something he hadn't noticed all day until now. But now he's seen it, he doesn't know how he has missed it ... there's an indicator alight on his father laptop, even though the lid's down. His dad never did that, never.

James goes over to the laptop while the others are all enjoying themselves arguing and throwing little tight tantrums. He opens the lid of the computer. It comes awake. The screen shows the last thing his father had been working on. The article stops half-way down the page, then this, written very large:

"I'm sorry - I can't take this any more!"

James stares at the screen. 'Look at this,' he says to the others, none of whom take the slightest notice of him. He reads the words again.

'Look!' he shouts out, turning to face them all. The room falls silent. 'Look at this!'

Everyone gathers round the screen. It seems to take a long time before anyone reacts, before the policeman finally decides to say, 'Well! Well, well, well.'

Three

Sandra

'And is your mother contactable?' the policewoman wants to know.

They're convinced by that message on the screen, the police and Mrs Pearce. They're sure now that Maria and James's father has run off somewhere. They reckon it won't be long before he comes back, once he's cooled down enough to think more clearly. The policewoman spends a long time trying to explain to Maria that people under a lot of pressure sometimes behave irrationally.

'It doesn't mean they don't care,' she tells Maria, 'quite the opposite. It's because they care so much that they're under so much pressure in the first place. You do see that, Maria, don't you?'

'You're wrong,' Maria insists. 'I know him. He wouldn't just run off like that, I know – '

'How about your mother, Maria?'

'How about her?'

'I understand from Mrs Pearce that your mother and father are separated?'

That Mrs Pearce! Sticking her nose in on everything that was nothing to with her, as usual!

'They're divorced. My mother's an actor.'

'Is she now?'

Mrs Pearce is still there, making tea in the kitchen, doing her bit. James is having a lesson from the policeman on how to work the radio he carries and what it's like to arrest somebody. James likes the idea of arresting people. He wants to find out how you go about getting people thrown in jail, in case he needs to know in future.

'An actress, you say?'

'No. An actor.'

'Ah. Yes. An actor. Would I have seen her in anything at all?'

'I don't know. I don't think so. She gets a lot of work in the theatre – small travelling companies. Do you go to the theatre much?'

'No. Never. I don't really get the time.'

There's a pause between them, in which James presses a button on the policeman's radio. It crackles into life. James is quickly relieved of it by the man, who switches it off and puts it away. 'Now I'm going to have to arrest you,' he tells James.

'And is your mother contactable?' This is the second time of asking. Maria ignored the question first time round.

'No.' Maria looks down.

'Oh. But surely – '

'I don't know how to contact her.'

The policewoman gazes at Maria for some while. 'Actors have agents, don't they? The agent would surely know where she is.'

'Yes, sure. But the details – everything's in Dad's diary.'

'Ah. And where's his – '

'On the computer. Everything's on the computer.'

'Can you show us?'

'No one can get into that diary. I can get into the file system, that's easy, but that diary's doubly secure.'

'Well, that's not very practical, is it?'

'He's a computer man. Computer crazy.'

'Perhaps we can find a way?'

'He used to write security software with Uncle Peter.'

'Uncle Peter?'

'He's not our uncle really. He used to be my dad's business partner. We wouldn't get into that diary in a hundred years.'

'Well, maybe we'll get one of our experts on it, if need be.'

'You can try.'

'If need be. But I'd have thought he'd have given you access, at least.'

'You might have thought so. You might have thought I'd be able to talk to my mother. You might have thought so, but I can't, can I?'

The policewoman allows another pause. 'And that hurts you, doesn't it, Maria?' she says, softly.

'She's in France at the moment,' Maria hurries the conversation along, 'in France in some small-time production. We have to wait for her to call us. She pretends she's missing us. But she really is an unbelievably bad actor. It doesn't matter. She doesn't ever want to know, not really.'

'Oh, surely she – '

'You don't know anything about it! Mind your own business, can't you?'

'It is my business, Maria. I'm a policewoman.'

'Yes, well I've told you we don't know how to contact our mother, so what are you going to do with us? Lock us up?'

James, over the other side of the room, wants to be locked up, especially with handcuffs on.

'Of course we're not going to do that, Maria. Don't you have any other relations living nearby?'

'No. We have an aunt in America. That's all.'

Then out comes Mrs Pearce from the kitchen, bustling through the door in her busy tracksuit, carrying a tea-tray loaded down with cups and plates and buttered bread and all kind of merry picnic stuff. She's placing the tray on the table, aware that she's being watched. Maria knows the police, both sexes, are observing Mrs Pearce doing her caring thing. She, Maria, knows what they're thinking, the police and Mrs Pearce herself – while Maria's thinking, Oh no, not that - anything but that!

She sighs to herself. Maria just knows that they're going to ask Mrs Pearce if she'd be so good as to take care of the children in need. Mrs do-gooding Pearce, always wanting to get a hand in their father's affairs, she'd agree like a shot. Nothing would please her more.

Which becomes self-evident when they do ask her. She flaps and fawns, caring and corny enough to make Maria feel quite sick. But she doesn't get a say in the matter, because all the others, including dumb James, think it's the only solution. They are going to have to stay at the Pearce's house with Sandra and her mum until their father turns up.

'It'll only be for a few days,' the policewoman assures Maria, 'I promise.'

'Oh, you promise, do you? That's all right then. What happens if you're wrong?'

'Let's just wait and see, shall we? We'll inform the authorities, Mrs Pearce.'

That good woman breathes in deeply in a flush of sacrifice and pride.

'Can I bring my games consul?' asks James, raring to go. Maria despises him for it. It's all a game to him. He's actually enjoying the prospect of a few days at the Pearces'! Maria would rather stay in her own house alone. But the police won't hear of such a thing. The house needs to be secured, they insist, and Mrs Pearce must keep the keys.

'You can have the spare bedroom, James,' Mrs Pearce tells him as soon as she has them alone in her clutches. 'And you'll be sharing Sandra's bedroom with her, Maria,' she says, as if that's supposed to be something good. Maria doesn't suppose so. In face, she thinks the opposite – Sandra's just about the last person alive she wants to share a bedroom with.

'Can't I share with James?' she asks the tracksuit.

'But he's a – he's a boy!'

'Well?'

'And you're a girl!' She looks like someone has tried to give her a punch in the face.

'He's my brother.'

'Oh no. Oh no, no, no. I couldn't possibly allow – it's out of the question. Go and put your things in Sandra's room, Maria, that's the best thing all round. Sandra will be home soon.'

Maria sighs deeply, picking up her bag of belongings. James is already away up the stairs. He's okay, he's fine – he doesn't have to share with anybody.

'And try not to touch any of Sandra's things,' tracksuit Pearce calls after Maria. 'She doesn't like her things being touched.'

Maria sighs again. She goes into Sandra's bedroom and chucks down her stuff onto one of the two twin beds. Maria hasn't been in here for years, but she knew what it was going to be like – bad posters, boy bands, poser pictures of haircuts and silly, sultry looks sideways at the camera. Sickening!

The bed on the right is Sandra's, Maria remembers, so she chucks all the stuff off the other one onto the floor. She can't believe the sort of junk Sandra has kept – teddies, stuffed doggies, an old doll, all laid out and sitting silent and sinister, but still sweet enough to give you tooth decay just looking at it all. The whole room's like this, pink and pretty – everything, in fact, that Sandra is not. Look at it! It's Sandra all over – sickly-sweet and superior, complacent and comfy, like a pink tongue poked out at you from a head full of nothing but its own sense of self-importance.

When Sandra gets home from school, Maria keeps well out of the way while Sandra's mum fills her in on the story. Maria doesn't want to have to listen to them, to watch Sandra's face through it all. In fact, she doesn't really want to ever have to look at Sandra's pudding face again for the rest of her life. Or listen to that wail of a voice.

Like now, as it whines and whimpers, what with Sandra having been upstairs, having clumped back down heftily complaining, crying, 'She's chucked my things all over the floor, she has!'

Maria's watching TV downstairs with James, pretending not to have heard.

'All my best things, all over the floor off the bed. All over everywhere, Mum! She's done that, she has!'

James is watching his sister as Maria still pretends to have heard nothing. James has got that look on his face, which *has* to annoy Maria, because of the way he lets things affect them. He lets Sandra and her wailing become important that much sooner than it needs to be. James is like a reflection of the wrong Maria is supposed to have done. It's no wonder she has to tell him where to go.

'Get lost, James.'

He doesn't, though. He's too thick. He just sits there ogling, with that sad scared look on him, the sort of expression Maria's never going to let anyone see on her, ever. Maria isn't going to give in to it. She doesn't respond as Sandra bursts in, flapping and flopping in front of the TV screen.

'You've slung my things all over the floor – she's slung my things all over the floor!' she points at Maria but looks at her mother she appears at the door.

'Have you slung her things all over the floor?' Mrs Pearce also points at Maria. 'Have you? Even after I asked you particularly not to?'

'I thought – ' Maria stops herself. She was going to say that she'd thought in was just rubbish, junk on the bed, getting in her way.

But Sandra's mum and Sandra are on at her, barking like a couple of hyenas, their mangy backs up.

'I specifically asked you not to!'

'She's – all over the – Mum!'

'I know.'

'But Mum!'

'I know, Sandra, I know. Maria, you're to go upstairs right now and pick everything up and put it all back where it belongs. Do you hear me?'

'But it's in the way.'

'Tell her I'll move it out of the way,' Sandra says to her mum, spitting venom at Maria. 'Tell her.'

'Sandra'll move it out of the way.'

'Well why can't she pick it up from where it is? It's only junk, anyway.'

'Mum!' Sandra's going into some kind of spasm, as if Maria just stuck a pin in her.

Maria's wishing she could do just that. And James is no use whatsoever, either. He's gone back to watching the television, that's how interested he is. Nothing holds his attention for very long. It really annoys Maria sometimes, the way nothing gets to him, as if he doesn't care about anything much.

But Maria cares. She cares too deeply. She's weighed down by so many things – the way people want to keep getting at her, at school, the teachers, at home, her father. And here, Sandra and her mother taking turns to stab at her with their sharp, shrill words.

'You WILL do it. You WILL do as you're told. As long as you're under my roof, you'll obey my rules and conform to my – to my – rules. Is that clear, young lady?'

Maria just gets up and goes out. As she's picking up all the cutesy and cuddly toys, she can still hear Sandra and that mother of hers harping on and on. At one point, she hears that woman saying to James, 'At least you're all right, Jamie.'

Jamie, she calls him! Nobody called James that, nobody. But what does she hear from the boy, in response? – Nothing! Maria pictures him munching digestives in front of the TV screen, no problems.

Well Maria has problems enough for both of them. She suffers here, even when everyone has fallen silent. They have dinner, but nobody speaks very much. Everyone's being over-polite as they sit round the table, with Maria and Sandra on opposite sides, trying not to look at each other. Maria feels as tense as a dry stick. She hates having to chew in a room that's too quiet, when all you can hear is the sound of other people chewing, knives and forks tapping and scraping on plates, the air gushing in and out of everyone's nostrils.

Then, afterwards, Sandra has to go and make a big issue of the homework she has to do. The way she talks about it is designed to let Maria know that at least *she's* been to school today, unlike some she might mention.

'Maybe you two should work together tonight?' Mrs Pearce suggests. It's met with a positive thud of disapproval from both girls. But Sandra complies, agreeing with her mother's suggestion, always wanting to be seen to be the cooperative one.

Maria doesn't mind at all being seen to be the uncooperative one. She doesn't mind that one bit.

'But you must keep up with your school work,' Mrs Pearce insists, when Maria refuses to have anything to do with Sandra's school work. 'If you don't, you'll be finding yourself even further behind than – '

She stops herself there, Mrs Pearce, having already said more than she'd meant to let out. Far more.

Maria has to wonder what this busy woman has been told about how Maria's doing at school. She looks over at Sandra, who slips her a sickly sweet smile.

'Anyway,' Mrs Pearce goes on, 'you must be sure to keep abreast of everything, mustn't you, Maria?'

'I've only missed one day. I'll be back there tomorrow. I'll read, upstairs.'

'But I'll be up there doing my homework,' Sandra whines, looking doe-eyed and pathetic at her mum. 'She'll be in my way, I know she will.'

'I'll only be reading,' Maria tries to speak directly to Sandra.

But Sandra will only communicate through her interpreter now. 'I have to have my music on, Mum. You know I can't concentrate properly without my music on.'

'Can you concentrate with Sandra's music on, Maria, do you think?'

'I don't think I can breathe with Sandra's music on, let alone concentrate,' Maria tells them. They leap, a couple of decent-sized pins in their backsides. Maria continues, before they can say anything. 'It's all right. I'll just watch the television for a while before bed. I wouldn't want to disturb Sandra at her homework, not for anything.'

She turns quickly and walks away, onto the other room where James is already watching TV. But he's just flicking through the channels using the remote – something he was never allowed to do at home. Round and round the channels he's going, one thing, the next, the next.

Maria dumps herself in the armchair. She can hear the dinner plates being gathered by a woman in a tracksuit, then a smug daughter's music starting upstairs, a boy band bouncing through their sing-along lyrics.

'It's all right here,' James suddenly says, without looking at her, 'isn't it, M'ria?'

She looks at him as he gazes at the flicked-through television programmes. 'Do you know what, James?' she asks.

'What?'

'You really are a loser.'

Still he doesn't look away from the TV screen.

'And stop messing about with that thing!' she shouts.

'I can't find anything good on.'

'I don't care. Leave it on one side or the other. You know not to play about with it like that.'

'That's only when Dad's here.'

'Well, he's not, but I am. Leave it! Leave it on that. That'll do. It's all rubbish, anyway.'

James blinks at the screen a few times before saying to his sister, 'I want Dad to come back, M'ria, don't you?'

She doesn't reply. She's too annoyed, not just by James. She hates hearing that music upstairs, the clattering of the cutlery from the kitchen. And she's speechless about the absence of her father.

'Where do you think he's gone?' James asks, turning to look at Maria now.

'I don't know, do I? If I knew, I'd tell someone to go there and get him. Get us out of this dump.'

James keeps looking at her, while Maria ignores him as much as she can.

'You don't like anything, do you, M'ria,' James says. It's not a question, but a statement of fact.

'I especially don't like little boys who say dumb things all the time.' She looks away from him now, to the TV where a natural history programme is about to begin. Something about reptiles and amphibians, so the announcer informs them.

'That's all I need,' Maria sighs.

'Sounds good,' says James.

'What's that?' asks Sandra's mother, appearing in the doorway. 'What's coming on?'

'About snakes and lizards,' James tells her.

‘Oh, good. I always enjoy a natural history programme, don’t you, Maria?’

‘Love ’em,’ says she, dead unenthusiastic.

‘What a pity Sandra’s got so much homework to do,’ Mrs Pearce says, ‘she would have enjoyed this. It would have been so nice, all of us watching it together, wouldn’t it?’

‘Oh, yeah,’ Maria shakes her head.

Oh, yeah, she thinks, really nice, that would be. Everything’s so nice and cosy. Like Sandra’s nice and cosy pop music and her mum’s nice and cosy tracksuit – lovely! Everything’s lovely!

Only it isn’t, she thinks to herself, always to herself and for herself and no one else. Nothing’s lovely really. Not really. It’s all boring, or uncomfortable, or crappy. Or it’s just plain annoying. Their dad’s gone off somewhere without so much as a word to his children – and there’s Mrs Tracksuit sitting nice and cosy in front of the TV with her thin crinkly backside in a cushion with her fat-cat daughter turning up the volume of her nice and cosy pop just to get up Maria’s nose. And James, just to get up Maria’s nose, he’s there blinking at the screen like an idiot. He’s nothing more than a piece of clay anyway, some kind of malleable stuff that anyone, even the Pearces, can do what they want with. Look at him. He likes it here! He likes it everywhere. What’s the matter with him, the empty-head?

That’s how the whole evening passes, the three of them in front of the TV, with Maria eating herself alive, the tracksuit bringing in tea, biscuits, taking a tray up to Sah-

Sandra, who is not giving up the bedroom, her territory, for anything tonight.

Then, when it's time to go to bed, James trots off, cleans his teeth, runs up to the spare bedroom just as if he's always stayed there. Maria's got this dusty feel to her teeth, a flavour in her mouth like bad tea that she just can't get rid of. She's getting a slight headache, as if she already hasn't slept properly. She's know she's not going to, so the headache's only going to get worse.

When they're in their beds, herself and Sandra, Maria can already sense the bad night pressing in on her. She can feel Sandra over there in the other bed like a presence, another bad and dusty flavour. Maria can hear Sandra's breathing. It's like a sighing every now and then, as if she was the one really put out by the disappearance of Maria's dad.

Maria lies silent and tense in her bed, listening to the Sandra-ness of her sighing surroundings. She knows Sandra's just about to speak to her, she can feel it. Maria lies there trying to give Sandra the feeling that she doesn't want to speak to her. It's the last thing she wants right now. But Sandra starts sighing, unable to feel through her thick skin Maria's reluctance to talk.

'Funny about your dad,' Sandra's voice comes out of the darkness.

Maria doesn't answer, because she hasn't so far been asked anything.

'Isn't it? Funny about your dad?'

'Yeah. Very funny. I can't stop laughing.'

'No, I didn't mean funny like that.'

'Didn't you?'

'No. You know – strange. Strange, isn't it, the way he just disappeared like that? It makes you wonder why, doesn't it?'

'Mmm.'

'It makes you wonder,' Sandra goes on, her voice quieter now, more whispery, more mysterious. 'It makes you wonder why,' she barely breathes the words.

But they enter straight into Maria's open ear. She had been expecting Sandra to wonder where – where had he disappeared to? Where could he be? But no – Sandra has to put the why question, the very thing that's been nagging at Maria the whole day. This is the very question that would have to suggest to Maria that it was all her fault, that she was the reason, the only reason he'd have gone off like that.

All day Maria had been trying to avoid that question. Now Sandra had to, had to bring it out, to hang it there in the dark like an awful accusation.

'Still,' Sandra says, more brightly, 'I expect he'll be back soon No need to worry. My mum reckons he won't be away for long. She thinks he just needs a break. Well, anyone would really, wouldn't they?'

'Shut up, Sandra,' Maria has to tell her. 'Just shut up, will you?'

'I was only saying.'

'Well now you've said, so shut up.'

'This is *my* house. I *can* say.'

‘This *is* your house, but it’s *my* father you’re talking about, and it’s none of *your* business. So shut up, will you, Sandra? Just shut up.’

Four

Grant

Even though she doesn't feel like to go to school next day, Maria's up early, leaving Sandra sleeping there in her bed with her mouth open and her smelly breath hissing out like a snake with adenoids.

Sandra's mum tells Maria she's up early, as soon as she appears in the kitchen. 'Am I?' Maria says, as if she didn't know.

Mrs Pearce is wearing a different tracksuit. 'Couldn't you sleep?' she asks Maria.

'Couldn't you?' Maria asks. 'Or do you get up early to go running?'

All she gets is a quizzical look in reply.

'Never mind,' says Maria, gulping some tea and taking a single bite out of a slice of toast. She wants to get out of the house before she has to see Sandra. So she spouts some rubbish to Mrs Pearce about needing to see to a few things at school before lessons start. She gets another confused look from the woman in the jogging suit before escaping into the good fresh morning air.

It's cold in the street. That's good. It takes away the dizziness of having had such a bad night's sleep. The walking wakes her. Then it makes her realise how hungry she still is. Tea and a bit of toast was no kind of breakfast. Maria usually has fruit, yoghurt and cereal. And lots of it. Her stomach begins to rumble.

Maria thinks about going to the greengrocer's to buy some bananas and oranges, but it's too early yet for any shops to be open. At least, she imagines it is. She doesn't want to walk all that way then not be able to buy anything. Maria wants to eat.

The key is in her coat pocket. Her front door key. She feels it there, turning it over a few times. She's a fair way up the road by this time. Not too far, though. Not too far to turn round, go back, flit into the house for ten minutes or so. She's out so early there's still time. Just about.

It's exciting, approaching the house, walking quickly up the garden path, opening the front door. It feels as though she's been away for an age.

As the front door opens, Maria can smell the place. She'd forgotten how much she liked it. She breathes her home in. It's even better than she remembers.

With the door closed behind her, Maria finds her excitement's so great she can feel her pulse going. She starts listening for something. She's standing just inside the front door, straining to hear a sound, her heart racing. If there's any noise, any slight sound here, it could only mean one thing ...

But there's only silence. He isn't there. And Maria's annoyed with herself, because the place is just as empty as when she'd left it the day before.

'Dad?' she calls, annoying herself still further. The vacant spaces do not echo, but they do sound different as she checks out all the room, looking for any changes. He may have been back for something.

In his bedroom, nothing's altered. The wardrobe doors are still open from where she'd flung them wide yesterday morning. The clothes he has left behind are still hanging there undisturbed. There's still the same line of shoes on the wardrobe floor.

Downstairs, nothing. A dead silence. Maria unpeels a banana from the fruit bowl and stands looking at the computer, her father's laptop. It's switched off now, but left open. The big policeman did it. Maria's father never would. He always turned it off and carefully closed the lid, as if he had respect for his work tools.

Maria doesn't like to look at it like that, so she pushes the on button. The computer runs through its start-up procedure.

Then it stops, the screen asking for a log-on password. Maria reaches over and takes an apple from the bowl before sitting down in her father's chair at his desk. She taps in the password. "Eraserhead". He'd thought it was a secret, but Maria had watched him tap it out too many times. She's got a pretty good idea how to find her way round his filing systems too. She even knows the article he'd been working on the night before and what name it had been saved under.

Maria opens the document, runs through to the end, where she expects to see the message he'd left them. It isn't there. The article just stops mid-way. That means it hadn't been saved. And the police wouldn't have saved it before switching the system down. They'd made their pencil and paper notes, they were satisfied.

But Maria isn't. She sits staring, chewing thoughtfully on her apple. Her father never used the auto-save function. He liked to do it and then back everything up himself, which he did, every few seconds or so. It was a habit. Doing it helped him think. He'd get into a rhythm or writing, saving, writing, saving. He would never, ever have left his work – or that message – without clicking on the icon.

So maybe she's got it wrong, she thinks. Maybe it was some other document he'd had opened and Maria had confused the two. That was a possibility. She'd just have a look at anything with a similar title, just to be sure.

For some reason Maria badly needs to see that message again. She wants to re-read it, to have another last look at the final thing he did before collecting his clothes and walking out on them.

Document after document she checks, opening anything that resembles the title of the one she'd been so sure about. Nothing. Then nothing again. And again. This is becoming like an obsession now. Maria cannot believe that her father, in whatever state of mind, would have failed to save something he'd written. He just wouldn't do that!

It's not until she stops to peel herself an orange does Maria notice how the time has ticked on through her preoccupation. Nearly twenty-past nine it is, all of a sudden. She's already late for school.

She leaps up, dropping the orange, grabbing her bag, dashing for the door.

Gone half-past nine it is, more like twenty-five to ten by the time she gets there. The idea of not going at all has flitted through her mind several times. She'd rather have stayed at home. But – and it's obvious what the big but is, it's Sandra, isn't it? That loud-mouth's already there, Maria knows, bad-mouthing Maria for playing truant and for being a terrible guest in her house. Maria couldn't afford not to go to school. Just being there would be a defence in itself. It she stayed away, Sandra would have the whole day to herself, hours and hours to put herself about, slanderously whispering. That was Sandra. That's what she did.

Sticks and stones? Whoever said that names can never hurt me was either the biggest liar or the biggest idiot in the whole history of the world. Whoever it was, they had certainly never experienced Sandra Pearce or her bullying, bitter crew.

Maria just cannot be bothered to explain to her form teacher why she was so late, or why she hadn't been there the day before. She doesn't want to have to talk about it to anyone, especially not any of the teachers. They'd only want to start offering her their sympathy, making Maria feel as pathetic as they are, as most of the other kids are. So Maria just tells her she's been unwell, that she wasn't too good first thing this morning, but she feels all right now. Mrs Harrison, the form tutor, asks her to bring in a note from her parents. Maria tells her she will, tomorrow. She won't, of course. How could she?

All she can do is hang on. She sits through the morning's lessons, dizzy with tiredness. By lunchtime, she's ravenously hungry, dog-tired, confused and uncomfortable. She feels hot and cold, as if she's got the flu coming. Luckily, all through the morning, no one asks her any questions about the work she's supposed to be concentrating on. If they had, she couldn't have offered any kind of answer, because she didn't even know what kind of lesson she was in. All she really wants to do is to get something good to eat then go home and sleep in her own bed all afternoon and straight through the night.

At lunch, Maria begins to notice. Things are happening. People are looking over at her. She looks back at them, they look away. All over the place there are strange glances in her direction. At one point, she catches a glimpse of James, who's sloping by on the other side of the fence between the junior and Maria's school, looking more than a little bit miserable. Something's got to him, badly, to give him a look like that on his face. Usually, James was insult-proof, too wrapped up in his own little world to let things bother him.

What is it, with all these furtive glances from all over the place? What's going on?

But then it's obvious, as soon as Maria gets another look from Sandra, sitting smug in a ring of furtive glancing faces over the other side of the refectory. Hers is the only face that doesn't turn away when Maria confronts it. This is the two-faced face that's been busy all morning, stirring it. Maria suddenly feels slightly sick to think of what might have happened to James to so upset him. If he's that bad, Maria doesn't like to think of the effect it might have on her.

So she ignores the whole lot of them. Even those few that would normally be on her side, she blanks. She just can't be bothered with any of it. There's a place, a corner of the field she always goes to get away from everyone for a while. Usually she reads there, if she's got a good book, something to take her out of herself and all of this for a little while. It's always helped her feel better.

Not this time, though. As soon as has she has sat down, James is there beside her, saying nothing, tugging up handfuls of grass. He's not supposed to be there, on this side of the school fence, but Maria doesn't want to have to take notice of him. He's going to drag her further into things. So she blanks him as well, pretending to concentrate on the book in front of her.

But there's the sound of James as he tears the blades of grass, as he sighs again and again.

'Get lost James, will you?' she has to say, in the end.

'Nowhere to get lost to,' James replies.

'Get lost anyway. You're not allowed over here. What's the matter with you?'

'Nothing.'

'Well get lost then!'

James doesn't stop plucking grass, tossing it away all round them. 'It's that lot,' he says, eventually.

Maria sighs, closing her book. She hasn't read a single word, anyway. 'What lot?'

'Them.'

'Who? Who're them?'

'Ev'ryone!'

'Oh. Well, join the club.' And she opens her book again and continues pretending to read.

'They reckon,' James says, after another while of grass root-ripping, 'they reckon he's done a runner.'

Maria snaps closed the book again. 'What?'

'Dad,' James has tears springing into his eyes. 'They're all talking about it.'

'So?'

'They reckon he's done a runner in the middle of the night - '

'Well he has!'

'But because of us – because of us.' Tears are running out of him now. That would usually make Maria really annoyed with him. Today though, things feel different.

'Sit on your coat,' she tells him, 'or you'll get all wet. This ground's damp. That's it. It's the wrong weather for sitting out here, really. That's right. Now then – you mustn't let them get you down. They're bound to all want to talk about it.'

'But how do they all know, even in my school?'

'I'll give you one guess. It's her, isn't it, that fat lump Sandra.'

'Sandra?'

'Who else? You wait till I see her!'

'They're all saying he's done a runner - '

'Don't keep saying that!'

'They reckon he ran off because of you and me. They reckon he couldn't stand any more of you. You're a loner, they reckon.'

'Do they now?'

'Yeah. They reckon you're sad as well.'

'Oh, yes?'

'Yeah. A sad loner they reckon, that's why - '

'All right! All right! I know about all that stuff they reckon. And is that what makes you cry? These pathetic idiots can make you cry as easily as that?'

'I don't like it, what they're saying about us.'

'Well I couldn't care less.'

'And I hate that Sandra, now.'

'Good. So do I. There, we're all right, aren't we? Just don't listen to anything they've got to say about Dad. They don't know anything, any of them. They think they do. Sandra thinks she does. Her mum thinks she does. None of them know a thing. They're all cretins, the lot of them.'

They're silent together for a few moments in which James plucks another couple of handfuls of grass. Then, 'Maria?'

'What?'

'What's a cretin?'

'It's what Sandra and her mother are. And all that lot talking about us. It's what they are. That's all you need to know. Now get lost, and don't let them get to you. Just remember they're all cretins.'

Maria's acting as if she doesn't care, but of course really she does. She cares a lot. Sandra's got too much over her and she doesn't like it. But Maria's not going to say anything about it. She wants to just ride the storm until her father gets back. There's nothing else to be done about it.

But then there's this nasty little incident you just cannot ignore. Maria's making her way to an English lesson later on in the afternoon, feeling even more tired and confused than ever. Head down, she's aware of, yet trying not to pay any attention to any of the others all milling through or hanging about in the corridors. Maria's doing nothing but trying to get through the day. But then she's made aware of a group up ahead, that mob always bad-mouthing with big-mouth Sandra, laughing at things, whispering, looking, all that. And there she is, gloating, in the midst of things – Sandra, fairly glowing with it all.

'Look out,' one of the cronies whispers, 'here she comes now.' But the whisper is loud enough for Maria to hear, easily.

Maria looks up, only to see the whole wobbly oily bunch of girls and a few boys with their eyes fixed ready to stare her out. Maria tries to ignore them at first, walking right through them.

'Let the orphan get by,' one voice calls from the back.

Maria lets it go. She feels even more tired than before, as if there's some hefty horrible Sandra-style weight bearing down on her in a fat blanket. She feels as if she could just lie down on the floor in the corridor and sleep, right under their feet, in spite of their pathetic comments.

'Where you going, Maria?' another voice pipes up.

'She's looking for her old man,' a third voice joins in.

They all laugh. At that! They think that's funny! Maria has to stop, to take a look at their smiling cretinous faces. 'What is the matter with you lot? she asks.

'And what's the matter with you?' Sandra says.

'Nothing's the matter with me.'

'Oh no? That's not the way it looks to me.'

'I couldn't give a monkey's how it looks to you.'

Everyone laughs. Maria turns to go.

'And I don't like what you've been saying about me,' Sandra says.

Maria stops. She has to. What Sandra's saying feels like a smack in the face. She turns back. 'You don't like what I've been saying about you?'

'No, I don't,' - with her head held, looking down her nose, her mouth laughably small.

'You don't like, what *I've* been saying, about *you*! What about everything you've been saying about me?'

Sandra glances to her her right and left, checking the crowd round her. 'What?' she says, looking back down her nose.

'Oh, you haven't been talking to everyone about me and my – my old man, have you!'

'I've been telling them why you're staying with us, that's all.'

'That's all?'

'I've been telling them how you come in, throw all my stuff about, cheek my mum - '

'Your mum!'

'Yeah. My mum! I've been telling them what an ungrateful selfish piece of vermin you are, and it's no wonder your old man's gone off and left you to it. Who wouldn't?'

Looking at Sandra, Maria feels this wave of fatigue and nausea sweep over her. She's too hot. Her skin prickles. She'd always felt a bit sick whenever she'd had to look at Sandra, but this is much worse than normal. Sandra's the lucky one, Maria reckons, because she doesn't have Sandra to stare at. But still they stand there.

'Hit her!' a voice calls out.

Maria and Sandra stare all the harder. Sooner or later, if only for the sake of the crowd, one of them is going to have to start something.

'And I don't like what you've been saying about us,' Sandra says, using the word 'us' to keep the crowd well and truly on her side.

'What am I supposed to have been saying about you?'

'You know what you've been saying.'

'I haven't been saying anything about you.'

'Then why is your brother going about telling everyone you reckon we're all cretins.'

'I said that because you've been getting at him.'

'I haven't – but I will do if he calls me a cretin again.'

'You leave him alone!'

'I'll have him and all, if he calls me names,' Jimmy Bains chips in now, spotty cretin that he is.

'You leave him alone as well, Bains, or I'll - '

'Oh, yeah?' goes Bains.

'I'll get you,' Maria tells him. She's boiling now, still dizzy but not tired at all.

'Oh, yeah?' goes Bains again, by Sandra's side.

'But if she doesn't, Bains,' this other voice comes in, 'I will.'

Maria looks round. It's Grant. There he is, leaning against the wall, looking dead lazily into Jimmy Bains's face. Maria looks back to where Sandra's standing next to Jimmy Bains with a face on him now not so convinced it wants to get anybody.

'Oh, you're always standing up for her,' Sandra almost spits. 'What are you, a loner, like she is?'

Grant steps forward with this little smile on his face. He's got good black hair, wavy and sleek. 'Loner, am I?' he says, stepping up to Jimmy Bains, taking him by the shoulder. 'What do you say, Jimmy, eh? Loner, am I?'

Bains blinks, glancing at Sandra. She's sighing with impatience, folding her arms, resting her weight heavily on one leg, her head cocked to one side.

'So, what do you say, Jimmy?' Grant asks him, speaking close, real close to his face. 'Loner, am I, or not?'

Bains shakes his head.

Sandra tuts.

'What did you say, Jimmy?' Grant's fingers are pressing harder into Bains's shoulder.

'No,' goes Bains.

Grant lets him go, immediately dragging someone else out of the crowd by one arm, some other boy, one of those that had so far been providing some of the comments. 'And what do you say, mate?'

Grant's new mate shakes his head. Grant drops him. 'How about you?' he smiles at one of the girls. 'Do you think I'm a loner, Sharon?'

'No, I don't,' Sharon tells him, smiling back.

Sandra tuts again. Maria flicks her a grin.

'Does anybody,' asks Grant, smiling round the faces left there in the corridor that has nearly emptied out but for them, 'does anybody here reckon I'm a loner?' Grant holds out his arms to the small crowd. Even Sandra keeps her mouth shut. 'No? Nobody?' He glances at Maria before going back to Sandra.

Sandra's head's so far to one side now she looks as if she's just about to topple over.

'So,' Grant speaks directly at her, 'nobody here but you reckons I'm a loner.'

'I didn't - ' Sandra starts to say.

'And,' Grant interrupts her, 'you also reckon Maria's a loner. But she's with me, and I'm no loner. So neither is she, is she.'

Sandra just sort of breathes closed-mouthed into Grant's face. Her head's still miles to one side, her arms folded, weight on one leg as if she doesn't care. She cares.

'No,' Grant answers for her, 'she isn't. But I'll tell you what, Sandra – the fact that you think she is, and I am, that makes you a loner, right? Because no one agrees with you, right?'

Sandra's just staring into him. But you should see her face now – the state of it!

Grant smiles at her. Then he turns, says, 'Come on, Maria,' - and leads Maria away from the centre of the disappearing crowd.

They walk down the corridor together, ducking round the corner where they can be alone. Grant laughs.

Maria's smiling, of course. She feels so much better already, *so* much better.

Grant turns to look at her. He's smiling too. 'Was that good, or what?' He makes a couple of fists and thrashes at the air. 'I love it – I love it!' He leaps and he laughs out loud.

'Fan-tastic!' Maria joins in, laughing loudly too.

'I've been waiting to have a go at that blob,' Grant tells her, 'ever since I came here. The things she's said about me and you.'

'You and me?'

Grant laughs again. Maria thinks, Like, wow! He looks all right, you know – really, all right.

'Not both of us,' he says, 'together. Although, come to think of it … '

Maria's laughing, but blushing too, she thinks. She feels she is anyway, however much she hopes she isn't. 'No,' she says, out of embarrassed confusion, 'no, really, thanks very much for that. She really is a - '

'Yeah, I know what she is all right. What amazes me, is why all those others can't see it.'

'I know. Maybe they're must scared she might start on them.'

'Maybe. I don't know.'

'Anyway, look, thanks again. I'm going to be late for - '

'But is it true?'

'How do you mean?'

'About your old man, your father?'

'Depends on what you've heard. Look, I'm sorry, I've got to - '

'He's gone off? Left you and your brother to it?'

Maria stops. She's going to be late for her English lesson, she knows that. What Grant's going to be late for, she hasn't got a clue, but he doesn't seem to be bothered. He always appears to be in control. Doesn't matter what it is, Grant's cool all right.

'Yes, night before last.'

'Just, disappeared?'

'Yes.'

'Without a word?'

'Yes, but I - '

'And what are you going to do about it?'

'Do?'

'About him, your old man?'

'What can I do?'

Grant glances round, as if she has just said something he can't quite believe. 'What can you do? Find him. Let him know.'

'I don't get it.'

'What's there to get?'

'Let him know what?'

'Just let him know you're not going to allow him to go off like that. Let him know what a louse he's being.'

'But he isn't that. He's nice.'

'Yeah? Well, he hasn't exactly been all that nice to you, has he? Look at you.'

'What's wrong with me?'

'Besides being so pale, tired and worried, nothing.'

'Yeah, well - '

'Well? What are you going to do about it?'

'I don't know. What would you do?'

'I told you – I'd find him.'

'How?'

'Well, you know him better than anyone.'

'Yes, but I don't know - '

'What was it like when he left?'

Maria stops to think about it. 'It wasn't like anything. He just suddenly wasn't there.'

'No. I mean, your place. The house. What did he take? What did he leave?'

'He left a note.'

'Ah.'

'On the computer. It's been wiped off.'

'What did he take?'

'I don't know. Clothes.'

'Which? Smart? Casual? How much of each? Did he take much money? Has he got his cheque-book, his cards?'

'Hold on! Wait a minute. What are you, some kind of private detective or something?'

'No, but I've got a pretty good idea. What you need to do is go back and gather information. That hasn't been done yet. Go back home tonight.'

'I can't.'

'Why not?'

'Sandra's stupid mother.'

'Oh, yeah. Sandra. Bad luck.'

'The worst. We're going to be very late, you know.'

'I know. Just tell them the truth.'

'The truth?'

'Always tell the truth. It knocks them out.'

'What, that I've been out here, talking to you in the corridor?'

'No, that your father's gone missing and you're sick over it.'

'Oh, that.'

'There you are then. You can do what you want. Nobody's going to touch you. Go back to the house, tonight. I'll go with you, if you like.'

'What about Sandra? And her mum?'

'Sneak out. What time do they go to bed?'

'About ten. They did last night, anyway.'

'I'll see you outside your place at what, eleven? What do you say?'

'I don't know.'

'Look, find your old man. You want to find him, don't you? Good. Then give me your address.'

So Maria writes it out on a piece of paper and agrees to meet him there that late at night. Then she spends the rest of the afternoon worrying about it. Just as well there's not much left of the school day. Soon enough, it's time to go back to Sandra's, where she, Sandra, is home like a shot to prepare a welcome for Maria.

The front door is opened before Maria can knock, and there they are, Sandra and her sliver-thin prop, side by side, standing like a bat and ball waiting for the games to begin.

'I've checked,' Sandra's mum blurts out, as Maria glances back through the front door, watching James sloping by their own house. 'He's not back yet, your father. I'm sorry, but there it is.'

James follows Maria in. 'How long they going to be here?' Maria has to hear Sandra whispering to her mother.

Maria herself has been wondering the same thing. Just how long could this go on before Sandra's mum decides to contact the authorities to come and take them off her hands? Not long, she has to hope, stifled under the heavy silence that's descending on this house. Maria had been expecting more cross words, but this, this nothingness, is worse. Much worse. Even James is badly affected by it, by this meaty atmosphere of tension and by what has happened to him at school today. He doesn't even care what he watches on TV. He doesn't care if he can have a biscuit or not. Now, *that* is bad.

There's a kind of ball of near sickness that Maria has to swallow down the whole evening through. No mention's made of homework. Nobody does anything. Which means the four of them have to sit downstairs before dinner and after. Dinner's just something to be got through, to be got rid of. It brings bed-time that much closer. But only that much, not nearly enough. Maria wants to tuck them all away by about half-eight, so she won't have to endure any more poisonous glances from Sandra or disapproval from her mother. Maria wants out of this house, now, even if it were to mean waiting in the cold for Grant for two hours or more.

Instead, she waits more than two hours in that house, repressed by the bitter glances from sad Sandra and her sadder mum, suffering from her brother's sorry acceptance of everything bad happening to them.

Sitting amongst all this, Maria finds herself agreeing more and more with what Grant had said to her – *she* has to do something. And she is going to. Besides, the very thought of meeting with Grant at eleven o'clock at night sends her stomach turning, but now with excitement. It helps take away that sick feeling, if only for a while.

At nine, James goes off without a murmur, Maria at half-past. Sandra stays behind a while. Maria hears her, and her mother, sharing poisonous whispers behind the not-quite closed living room door.

Maria makes sure she's in bed by the time Sandra does come up. She lies hidden, facing the wall.

But Sandra, as soon as she comes in, says, 'I know you're not asleep.'

Maria ignores her.

'I'll get you for what you done today,' Sandra says.

'Did,' answers Maria.

'What?'

'What you *did* today. Your grammar's not up to much, is it?'

There's this long, long silence as Maria senses Sandra standing over her, spotty with rage. Maria allows herself a little smile. She knows now, with Grant's help, there's nothing Sandra can do to her. She's Sandra-proof. It's a good, good feeling.

Nothing more is said. Sandra's bed creaks, her angry blankets ruffle. She fidgets, then falls still.

Maria lies listening. She doesn't feel too tired now. More like excited, thinking about meeting Grant. But lying warm in bed in the dark waiting for the TV to go off downstairs, her eyes start to fall. She has to keep ducking under the bed covers to press the little button for the light on her wristwatch. Time's running even more slowly.

She stretches.

Sandra lets out a moan.

Maria pushes the covers off herself, trying to keep awake in the cold. But she's soon too cold, shivering. The time's never going to go.

But of course it does, as it always does. Maria doesn't fall asleep. Not for any longer than a few seconds anyway. She forces herself awake, again and again.

Then it's almost ten o'clock. But the TV is still on. Maria can make out the mumble of the dialogue from some film or series Sandra's mum's still watching downstairs.

Maria checks on Sandra. There are some very sloppy snores coming from that direction, so Maria slips out of bed and cracks open the door. She listens out. That film's still going strong. Maria slips back into bed with the door left slightly ajar so that she can hear more clearly. The film continues, on and on. Maria turns, listens. She turns again. She listens. She hears that film, people talking, non-stop.

Half-ten comes. Sandra's still emitting bad air from various different places. There's a kind of snotty whistle from Sandra's nose that Maria has to listen through for any sign of that film possibly ever coming to an end. It seems set to go on all night.

Half-ten goes, giving way to everything else. Eleven o'clock's coming on too strong now. Grant is due to appear. Maria shifts in her bed. Ten more minutes flicker by under the blankets in a glimmer of ghastly green wristwatch light.

On the screen downstairs, that woman's still weeping. Maria can feel Sandra's mum snivelling along with her. Sandra whimpers in her sleep. This whole house is starting to cry as Grant-time comes and goes. Maria needs to get out of here, now.

She get up, quietly dressing. The TV's loud enough to allow her to lope downstairs undetected, her shoes in her hand. It's eleven o'clock nearly – too nearly.

Maria white-socks past the open door, through which she can see the back of the head of the weeping woman on the settee watching the woman weeping on the screen. Maria has to get into the kitchen to lift the spare front door key from its place on the hook by the kettle. She slips in and swipes the key. She's going to go out through the back door, come back in through the front when everyone's sound asleep.

But her hand is barely touching the back door handle when she hears movement from the other room. The film's still on, but Sandra's mother's on the move, going to the loo, maybe. Maria hopes so. She ducks down next to the freezer, out of the way. She listens, hoping to hear footsteps thumping up the stairs. But no. The light snaps on in the kitchen. Maria shrinks. She listens. The kettle gets filled, switched on. Then the feet pad to the back door. The key in that door gets turned.

Crouching down now, Maria is looking up leopard-skin leggings to the top, where the woman wearing them stands staring out. Sandra's mother would only need to look to her left and down and she'd see Maria crouching there. Maria blinks up at her, her heart pounding out a drum-solo, cymbals and all. Mrs Pearce stands there, right there in front of crouching cringing Maria, gazing out of the back door window. Everything's pitch outside. There's nothing to look at, but Mrs Pearce studies it anyway.

Maria's mouth has dried out. Mrs Pearce rubs her left eye. The kettle clicks. If that woman turns round left, she'll definitely spot Maria. There's an awful eye-wiping moment that seems to Maria to have gone into slow motion, finishing with a lazy right turn of the head, as if Mrs Pearce has been shoved that way by the wiping of her eye.

Left like a stone gnome carved into place, Maria's still staring up into the place in the air that Sandra's mum has just vacated. Without the merest movement, Maria listens to the sound of coffee being made. The granules fizz in the cup under boiling water. It smells quite lovely.

Then the footsteps retreat, the light goes off and the door closes. Not until then does Maria allow herself to exhale completely.

In the new dark, Maria rediscovers her limbs. She unlocks the back door again, ignoring the cramps in her legs. Maria realises she's taking the risk of Mrs Pearce re-checking the door before she goes to bed. If she were to find it unlocked, Mrs Pearce might begin to suspect something. But it's worth taking a chance, because, well, she's off to meet Grant, isn't she.

But now it's well after quarter-past eleven. Maria has to run. Nearly twenty-past. He isn't there.

He isn't waiting for her in the street, he isn't hiding out in the garden. Maria hisses out his name. Nothing. It's eleven twenty-five. He's either been and gone, and she's missed him, or he never showed. She cannot know which. But she can't afford to hang about out here, running the risk of being seen. Maria has to let herself in the house, closing all the curtains before fumbling out into the kitchen where she's certain there's a hand torch.

The torch is huge and too powerful. It lights up everything. Maria only turns it on momentarily, to look at something specific.

How empty the house is, with silence filling all the vacant spaces. The emptiness is in all the things, exaggerated by the yellow light of the hand torch.

Their father has not returned.

Maria has come to check things, to look for clues as to his whereabouts. She shines the torch onto the computer screen. But she has already checked here. Nothing. Other than the fact that his message has been erased.

Now, what else did Grant say she should be looking for? Oh yes, his clothes. What has he taken, what has he left behind?

But peering into his wardrobe with the torch, it's not as easy as that. How is she supposed to remember what clothes he has? There are a few jackets left on hangers, the odd shirt. What's the meaning in that? Nothing, as far as she can see.

She hangs about, looking at the few things still hanging there, almost waiting for one of them to do something. Which is stupid. Maria's very quickly angered by it all. She slams the door, shuddering at the noise she's making.

But then, what was that she'd noticed, on the floor of the wardrobe, just as the door closed?

She re-opens it, shining the torch in and down.

Shoes. His shoes, all in a neat line, just as he always kept them. Four pairs. He has only the four pairs. And there they are. All four pairs.

What, has he gone away in his slippers?

In his slippers? Surely not!

So – where on earth *is* he?

Five

Maria and James

Dreaming, by the look of him. Little frowns and twitches flit across his face as his eyelids barely cover the eyeballs rolling underneath.

A hand crosses the torch-light beam to clasp him across the mouth. The lively eyes go still, then open, dilated but adjusting quickly to the too-strong light.

'Shshsh!'

James tries to shake his head, but Maria's grip holds him steady. 'Keep quiet,' she whispers, her face almost touching his. 'Will you keep quiet?'

She feels his head trying to nod. Slowly her hand peels away, a single finger at a time.

'What's the matter?' he hisses.

'I'm getting out of here.'

'What?'

'Shut up! Keep it down. Listen. I said I'm getting out of here - '

'Where you going?'

'Somewhere good. I'm going to get help. Something's happened to Dad, I'm convinced of it now.'

'What's happened to Dad?'

'Keep your voice down. I'm not sure what's happened, I just know something has. I've got to get help.'

'Who's going to help?'

'Uncle Peter.'

'Yes. Shall we go to Uncle Peter's?'

'We must. Are you coming, then?'

'Course. Let me get dressed.'

Maria waits for him, hurrying him, keeping him quiet. But already she's wondering why she's bothering to bring James, liability that he is. She'd be better of without him, the useless brat.

But she knows what it would be like for him to wake up and find his sister has disappeared too. She cannot bear to think of him having to suffer Sandra, in all her vindictiveness, with the effect all that could have on James in school. In the end, she has no choice but to take him with her.

Out again, into the cold and still night air. Maria has hung the door key back on its hook. They have squeezed the back door to, escaping round the side of the house and into the street. It's colder still. James is shivering. Straight away, he wants to know when they are going to get there.

'We've got to walk,' Maria snaps, as cold as he is. 'It's a long way.'

'Well why can't he come and pick us up?'

'He's not in.'

James pads along under the street lamps, his hands tucked up into his sleeves. 'How do you know he's not in?'

'I phoned him, from the house. He's not in.'

'Phone him again then.'

'No need. I know the way.'

'Oh.' He slaps along in his training shoes and his jeans. He's making smoke in the air with his breath. 'How far is it before we get there, then? How far do you reckon?'

'Look, James, shut your mouth, would you? Just walk. We've not even got to the High Street yet and you're getting on my nerves. Do me a favour, would you? Just walk.'

James trudges on, attempting to blow a smoke ring in the colder and colder air.

Maria watches him out of the corner of her eye. She listens to the way his jeans rustle as he walks. There's such a long way to go. 'Look,' she has to say to him, 'I don't really know how far it is to Uncle Peter's house. I only know it's a long way. We've only ever done it by car, you know that.'

'But can you remember the way?'

'Of course I can. Can't you?'

James doesn't answer. He never bothers answering Maria whenever he doesn't know something, to prevent her rubbing his nose in it. She's always sneering at him, calling him thick, just because he can't be bothered to remember the things she remembers.

In actual fact, this time Maria doesn't remember, either. She's got an idea she'll recollect the road-signs as they go along. She'll certainly know the street when they get there, the house in the street. She knows the area in which Peter lives – it's called Breckenwood. Maria's got a pretty good idea whereabouts it is from here. Yes, all in all, she's pretty sure she knows where she's going.

It should be easy, she keeps telling herself, because they did the journey in the car enough times when their father and Peter were in the computer software business together. Just after their mother left to go on tour, they were over there just about every day. Peter and their father were writing software for security systems, so the summer holidays had to be wasted hanging out round Peter's house, waiting for them to finish work for another day. James hadn't minded it too much as there were kids next door for him to mess about with, plus plenty of computer games. But Maria had been bored mindless. She'd read about nineteen, twenty books that summer.

But Uncle Peter was all right. He was good fun, a laugh. Especially after he'd had a few drinks. A bit of a nut-case, sometimes. Maria's dad always said it was because he'd never got married or had any children. Maria's dad always said Peter really ought to grow up. But he liked him a lot as well, despite the arguments they'd often have about their work.

Maria could never see what there could possibly be to argue about. But argue they did. Then sometimes they'd have some drinks afterwards. Sometimes, they'd have so many drinks, the old man couldn't drive home. They'd all have to spend the night, ordering a take-away for dinner. Which was okay, but it meant the two men could start work that much earlier the next morning, which meant a longer day for Maria to get bored in.

But there is no one else to turn to. Not now. And that's a pretty spectacular realisation. It bursts out on Maria's cold skin as she steers her little brother towards the High

Street. There is very nearly no one to turn to. Safety is so … tenuous. Is that the word? Tenuous seems right. There doesn't seem to be much safety left, certainly not in these icy streets leading to the main-road lamp-lights where a young girl and a younger boy on their own are bound to be conspicuous.

Midnight. Gone midnight. The High Street. Maria had been expecting it to be deserted, save for the odd nuisance nosey policeman. But it isn't like that, not at all. There's so much traffic moving still. And the people! After midnight, little gangs, boys mainly, young lads on parade, laughing. Couples wander up and down as if it's Sunday afternoon in the height of summer. Here and there a single young man or woman strides up and away, looking as if they've got to get somewhere urgently.

Maria had been expecting to have to dodge out of the way whenever someone came along or a car went by. Nothing of the kind. There are so many people about, so many Chinese restaurants and Kebab takeaways still open, that she and James just do not look out of place at all. James might be a little young, but no one seems to care.

She herself, Maria's surprised to discover, doesn't look at all too young to be out at this time of night. At one point, a boy's voice cries out, 'Maria! How's it going?'

A hand is glimpsed flapping from a car window, but Maria cannot quite see who's doing the waving. She can tell though that it's definitely someone of her own age, probably someone she knows from school. No wonder some of the boys looked so tired out during the day, up cruising till this late. No wonder so many of them never did any homework. Crazy. Maria doesn't like it. It's all too much, too soon.

James doesn't even notice. He's walking up the road as if he's just popped out with his sister for a packet of biscuits. Nothing ever really seems unusual for him. Maria can't help but watch him on the sly, fascinated by his lack of curiosity. He's playing games, blowing stuff up in his imagination, machine-gunning cars, all that funny stuff boys of his age do. Maria can't help feeling that if she'd been making her way up the High Street at this time of night with a younger sister, everything, everything would have been different. A whole new story.

But it's this story. It's cold. No sign of any rain, though. That's one good thing. One thing to be thankful for.

One thing, or several things, not to be thankful for, are making their way towards them. Maria notices this gang of mincers slicing down the road in sports gear, baseball caps with hoods over them. Some bunch of lads this is, judging by their loud mouths and the kind of language coming from them. Even James notices their approach and stops playing his little mind games.

There's a bike just up ahead, leaning against the railings by the road. One of the lads jumps on it and starts to ride around his mates, some seven or eight of them, as they try to slap him off. They're all laughing. The one riding the bike's doing a wobbler across the pavement in front of his little crowd. He has noticed Maria and James coming and begins directing the bike at them.

Maria shifts herself and James to the other side of the pavement. As she does, the lad on the bike changes direction, wheeling straight up to them before braking, forcing them to stop. Maria puts her arm around James's shoulder.

'Can't you see me ridin' my bike there?' says the lad.

'Excuse me,' Maria answers, trying to walk round him.

He shifts the front wheel of the bike into their path again. The rest of the gang are all gathered round now, peering out at Maria from under the peaks of their caps, from deep inside their shadowy hoods. There's cigarette smoke too, the real stuff, not James's ordinary cold exhalations of the air. There are eight or nine vague faces converging, none old enough for a proper shave, but all truing to look tough enough for a razor, spiteful behind their sharp smiles.

Maria makes an attempt to find a way through them. She fails. They close ranks. It is out of the question to turn back the way she has come. She holds harder onto James without knowing how he's reacting so far to this.

'Going somewhere, darlin'?' asks the one on the bike.

'Yes. My father's waiting for us, in the car, just up there.'

'Up there?' he says, this same one. He seems to be the spokesman. The others just stare coldly, blankly. 'Up there?' he says again, turning to look, one leg looped over the crossbar of the bike. 'Where up there?'

'Just round the corner. A bit.'

'Oh. Round the corner, is it? Where you been, then?'

'Nowhere. Just, collecting my little brother here.'

'Ello, little brother,' the spokesman says. He's the littlest but the loudest of the bunch.

'Hello,' James says to him.

'Hello,' mimics another. They all laugh.

James laughs.

'Please let us through,' Maria says, as soon as the laughter dies down. 'Our father's waiting.' She too has laughed – not because she felt like it, but because she felt it was the best thing to do at the time. She doesn't think she's in too much danger from this lot, but you can't be too careful. 'Excuse me,' she says again, trying to pick her way through. Most of them would have let her go. But the one on the stolen bike, he was different. He closed her off again with that front wheel.

'Don't rush off,' he says, most politely. 'You haven't even told us your name yet.'

'It's – Maria. What's yours?'

They all laugh again. One whistles, with smoke coming out of his mouth.

'Me? My name's Leroy. Leroy Ignatius Rockafella the Third. Ever heard of me?'

'No. Should I have?'

'Yeah. Me and my bike here.'

'That's not your bike,' Maria is dismayed to hear James say.

'Oi!' spits Leroy, if that's really his name. 'Watch what you say to me, little big-mouth.'

'I bet it's not,' James says.

'Shut up, James,' Maria tells him.

'And I bet you're not even old enough to smoke,' James points at the whistling one with his cigarette.

They all laugh again. All except the one smoking. He doesn't seem to find it funny at all. 'Watch it, kid,' he threatens.

'He is old enough,' the leader on the bike interjects. 'Do you know why he's old enough, little James?'

James shakes his head.

'He's old enough, because you can smoke at any age. Didn't you know that?'

'No.'

'No, I didn't think you did. Even you're old enough to smoke, James – isn't that right, lads?'

They all agree with him. Of course they do.

'See?' he says, grinning. 'So, do you smoke, James?'

'Of course he doesn't!' Maria holds him tight.

'Don't you, Jamie?'

'I don't. And my name's not Jamie.'

'Why don't you?'

'I don't like it.'

'How do you know if you've never tried it?'

'He doesn't want to try it,' Maria says.

'Let him speak for himself. What do you say, Jamie – James?'

'I don't want to try.'

'Give him a drag, John,' Leroy tells the smoker.

'I don't want to!'

'Leave him alone. Come on, James.'

'Stop them, boys,' Leroy instructs the gang, jumping off his stolen bike. 'Get hold of them.'

'Let me go!' Maria demands. Two of the boys are dragging her arms back, two others holding hard onto James.

'Shut your face!' Leroy snaps at Maria. Then he bends down to where James his his mouth clamped shut. 'Give me a fag, John,' Leroy says, taking one from the other boy's packet.

John lights it for him using a box of matches. Leroy breathes in smoke, before blowing it into James's face. James turns his head.

'Leave him alone!' Maria shrieks, struggling to get free. The boys are laughing, but gripping her tight. 'Leave him!'

James is having his head forced, face forward, his cheeks clasped to open his mouth in an o-shape. His eyes are wide, straining to see his sister.

Maria is watching him to see how he's taking it. She has stopped shouting in case it panics him. So far, he's doing okay. He isn't giving in. His face is set tight against what they're trying to do to him, but there are no tears in his eyes. Not yet.

The cigarette is shoved between James's lips, held there. James spits, coughing. The gang of bullies are all laughing.

'You cowards!' Maria shouts out, which only makes them laugh all the more.

Now there's a tear escaping from James's screwed-tight eyes. He cannot breathe properly. He's starting to panic, to go stiff, tightening up with terror.

'Let him go now,' Maria asks them, speaking up through their loud and spiteful laughter. 'Can't you see you're hurting him?'

'Just about the right size for you, Daniel, I expect,' a man's voice comes, as if from nowhere.

The laughter cuts. Both Maria and James are dropped in an instant. James dashes into Maria, burying his face against her. She hugs her brother, looking up at the man who has appeared so suddenly.

'Don't move, any of you,' the policeman says. 'Don't you dare move a muscle. Well, well, Daniel Davis and the boys. What a right little crew. Shut up, Davis. I don't want a word from you, unless I ask for it. Right?'

Daniel Davis (Leroy Ignatius Rockafella the Third) nods.

'What did you say, Davis?' demands the policeman.

'I said okay, Mister Fry.'

'That's good. Now then,' he says, turning his gaze to Maria and James huddled together there, 'I'd guess this isn't exactly what you'd call fun, is it, Miss?'

'No,' Maria agrees, 'not exactly.'

'It's okay, you're quite safe now. You all right, young 'un?'

The young 'un, James, nods up at him.

'Bit late out, aren't you?'

'Yes. I've just come to collect my brother – from our uncle's. Our father's just fetching the car.'

The policeman glances round. 'Where is he?'

'Oh, he's round the corner. Just up there.'

The policeman takes a look over his shoulder. 'Up there?'

Maria nods.

'Okay. You're all right, are you?'

Maria nods again.

'Did they hurt you, young 'un?'

James shakes his head, swiping the tear from his cheek.

'Go on, then, get going. - Not you lot! Stay right where you are. Now then ... '

Now then, and Maria and James are off up the street out of harm's, and the law's, way. They walk, faster, faster still, trying to resist the urge to run. Maria can just make out the policeman asking the lads whose bike that is lying across the pavement.

As soon as they can, they turn off the main road into a quieter side street. 'That was a close one,' Maria breathes.

'I wasn't scared, though,' James says. 'I wasn't – were you?'

'I was just afraid the policeman would try to stop us,' Maria says. 'Let's try to keep to the side roads from here on, shall we? It'll take a bit longer, but we'll be safer keeping more out of the way. If we see anyone coming, we can dodge behind a parked car or in a garden or something, okay?'

And so they make slow progress, hiding away at the first sound of footsteps. The moon is out and full, small but bright in the clear sky. Wherever there are no street lamps, the hard white moonlight illuminates everything like a flat cold, slightly dimmer sun. And cold it is, that moon's reflected light, exaggerating the cold, as if there's frost contained within it. Sounds seem to travel too far. A cough goes out to the whole neighbourhood.

That's how they come to hear the shout so early. 'There they are!'

The voice carries up the frost-bitten street.

Maria and James look round. Scattered shadows shift under the far street-lights. The old gang are there, running, Daniel Davis and his boys, broken free from the short reach of the law.

'There they are!' the cry echoes down the empty street.

And there they go, Maria and James, with one quick glance over their shoulders, galloping round the corner.

'Oh no!' Maria hisses.

'They're gonna get us, M'ria! They're gonna get us!'

'No they're not. Run!'

They run. You bet they do. Maria guides them round another corner, then another. She figures the more choices she gives them, the less likely they are to make the correct one.

'Keep down,' she tell her brother. 'Run next to the cars. Keep down!' All this as they run the length of another long road. It's murder to have to keep going so straight, without the benefit of another corner to hide round. Maria can sense the presence of all the yobs in the world, all breathing smoke down their necks. As they run past a bike, Maria imagines the gang following close behind stealing it, running them both to ground under its front wheel.

At last, at long last, a corner comes. But not until the end of the next street is reached do Maria and James realise that it comes to a sudden dead end. They've run themselves into a little cul-de-sac. There are a dozen or so big houses standing round a little green, as if crowding in on and peering down at brother and sister as they gasp for a breath of air.

'Quick!' Maria drags James into one of the front gardens where the hedges hem them round, particularly dense and black. That white-hot freezing moon up there casts great thick shadows by the bushes. Once in, it's as if Maria and James have be swallowed up, gone.

They want to stay there for a long time, safely out of harm's way. They want to sit tight, but the grass under them crackles, the very soils creaks. F-f-f-frozen, temperature falling, f-f-f-falling, every second or so it seems. The moonlight appears like snow on the ground. That's because it almost is. The snow that creeps up on a clear sort of night like this, with white crystals forming, climbing up every blade of hardened grass. F-f-f-frost.

'I'm f-f-f-f- '

'So'm I, M'ria.'

Crouched there side by side, they shift every now and then to prevent their ankles going to sleep under them. The dead leaves crack against their soles.

The sleep attacking their ankles seems to climb up their limbs, like crystallized cold rising. One at a time they nod off for a moment, before the cold slaps them awake again.

Mara cannot help but long for the warmth and the comfort in that little spare bed in Sandra's room. It feels like remembered heaven compared to this frozen-over hell.

James sways and then topples, with his arms round his scrunched up legs. He crashes into the snap-backed leaves and lies their curled and crying like a hedgehog who's forgotten how to hibernate.

'Come on,' Maria tells him, picking James up by the spines down his splintery back. 'We can't stay here.'

'But what about that lot?'

'We've lost them, I'm sure. I haven't heard anything, have you? They're gone. Let's go.'

'Which way, though?'

'James, this is a dead end. There's only one way to go.'

'I mean after that.'

'I'll know,' Maria insists, leading him away. But the truth is, she doesn't know. Not now, even if she ever did. There are no signs. She doesn't want to go back the way they came, that's all. The other way, away from the gangs of boys, will be best for them.

It goes some way, the other way. All the way to where they do not want to go, it goes. It dumps them somewhere very like the place they've tried to escape from. Another main road opens out, orange under its wash of arc lights. There are no shops here. The road is so big, it has a crash-barrier running down its centre like a spine. The motors hiss up and down this fairway, doing what looks like a ton.

Maria and James watch for a while, wondering where all these cars could be going. They don't know where *they're* going any more, except that they need to get away from here right now. The danger of cars this time of night, under this many madly illuminating street lamps, is the people contained in them. Maria and James will be seen walking here, traipsing cold and tired and hungry along a road that leads, surely, to where only late-night cars could wish to go.

They cut back into the maze, the labyrinth of residences. So many houses lie in so many roads. Maria cannot continue to make all the decisions. Her mind is too tired, her body too cramped to let her think about things any more. She asks James where he thinks they should go now.

'How should I know?' he says. 'Don't you know?'

'Of course I do,' she lies. 'I just wondered if you did, that's all.'

She's exasperated at herself, asking him something like that. This is James, the idiot little brother who always refuses to accept any of the responsibility and bad feeling of being the older sister and being lonely.

A catch of emotion clicks in Maria's throat as that thought occurs to her. She doesn't necessarily think of herself as being lonely. It's just that thinking about being lonely saddens her, welling up from her tightened stomach. She wishes she had seen Grant tonight. She feels sure, had she met him outside the house as planned, she and James wouldn't be trudging through the lost streets now.

Deep inside her own thoughts, Maria leaps as James, right by her side, practically screeches into her ear. Maria trampolines forward.

'Garniss,' some red-nosed dirty old man's sneering, his hands reaching out for them. 'Garniss,' he slobbers.

Maria, made aware of the red bead of a lit cigarette end, drags James away. 'Run!' she shouts.

Shouting run like that is a totally unnecessary thing to do, as James is on the sprint already. He too has got the drunk's cigarette stench up his nose. He's ahead of Maria.

'Garniss! Shay!' the drunk is yelling. He's slipping and sliding after them, his wobbly legs as if on ice.

'That way!' Maria ties to direct James. 'Not down there, down here!'

They scramble down a grassy bank together, diving through a line of trees at the bottom, then out into an open playing field. The frosty grass crunches under their feet as they dash for the other side. Behind them, a thud, a gasp, a last cry as the drunk goes over, his legs above his head, sliding down the green bank on his back, into the line of trees.

Maria and James can hear that he has fallen, but they don't take any chances. They aren't going to stick around to see if he gets up again. They're off, way across the far side of the field, through a few more trees, up onto a little dirt track by the canal.

It's dark. Something rustles in the bushes. James flies away from whatever it is, fleeing in one direction, Maria in the other. In a moment they've lost each other in the bushy dark.

'Maria!' James starts to shout at the very top of his voice. 'Maria! Maria! Maria!'

'James! Stay where you are.'

There's another rustling in the bushes. Maria rushes by the sound, following the line of the canal. Her skin is crawling. Unseen things are creeping after her.

She dashes by another clump of bushes, glancing round to try to spot what's closing in on her. Then thump, she runs straight into it.

For a moment or two she fights. But then she realises she's fought with this one many times in the past. It's James, who screeching, 'Maria! Maria! Maria!' He's lashing out at the thing he thinks is attacking him.

'It's me!' she shouts into his face. 'James! It's me!'

'Oh!' he's squawking. 'Oh! Oh! Oh!'

Maria shakes him. 'Enough! Come on! Quickly. There's something down there in that bush. Move! This way. No, this way! Hold my hand. Now run. Run!'

James feels a brush against his legs. He cries out. Maria cries out. They dash away from the canal, through another line of trees, through a broken gateway and into a yard. There's a screech behind them. They run harder, driving themselves back into civilisation, to the sanctuary of an old decrepit caravan parked, or rather dumped, at the far end of the yard. It looks, to them, like some kind of temporary home, an indoors they might own for a while. Inside they could hide from the night, from the dead hard shadows that harbour everything that wants to chase them.

The caravan boxes them away from all that the instant its manky old door slams behind them. There's a broken window admitting a slant of moonlight. It lies on the floor in a triangle. But for that, the darkness is complete.

Nothing rustles here and the frost is kept outside, although it is still freezing. The still, indoors air allows Maria and James to breathe more calmly.

Without a word, they move together, crossing to the busted window. Outside, nothing moves. All is silent. There are no more drunks, no more yobs, no lit cigarettes. This is a proper sanctuary. It is rest, for a while, maybe until the morning. On a frostless floor, at least they could lie down.

Then, what was that? Another rustle? They tense, the two of them, peering through the half-open window for any signs. But everything seems quiet out there. Dead still. Nothing.

BANG!

Straight out of the chill stillness, their shoulders, Maria and James, both grasped. Bang! A heavy hand, one on each. They freeze. Nowhere to go now. Now they're cornered, caught. They stand frozen to the spot, waiting for the worst.

A rasping breath tears the air between their heads. The stench from it wipes their faces with hot heavy moisture. A laugh cuts them to bits. A laugh, flecked with phlegm, spats against the remaining plastic glass of the window.

Then a voice rasps out. 'I'm Old-Fashioned,' it says.

Six

Old Fashioned

They wail, you bet. You bet they scream. But the place doesn't come down. They run for it, but now with nowhere to go, trapping themselves in the other end of the caravan, thumping the walls, crying to get out.

There are no exits for them, surrounded as they are by putrefied air too obviously chock-full of hideous after-breath and deep armpits and it doesn't do to think of what else.

Inside with Maria and with James, as they cower and crow in the darkness, a shadow like a big blown overcoat cackling through gobs of spittle.

'Let us go!' Maria screams out.

'I'm old-fashioned,' the spectre cackles.

'Let's run for it,' James suggests, through his bumpy breath.

'He's by the door,' Maria whispers. 'He's got us trapped down here.'

They cling to one another, crouching in the far corner. The shadowy tent-coated ogre shifts out of the leaking moonlight. For moments on end, massively elongated, buttock-tightening moments, neither of them can see him. James lets out a squeak.

Then a match ignites, illuminating a big bearded, black-toothed face next to the only exit door, with masses of grey hair floating out from everywhere. The match light sets fire to another, bigger flame. A gas ring is set ablaze, blue with watery, shifting shadows across the walls. The big-coated apparition cackles over the flames.

'I'm old-fashioned.'

'Let us go,' Maria pleads now.

The thing laughs itself into another coughing fit, coughs away until the laughter returns. 'I'm old-fashioned.'

'What's he going to do with us?' James whispers.

'I don't know. Keep quiet. I think he's mad.'

Under the old camping stove that lights this madman's house, a whole jumble of rags and papers, packets, tins, wrappers, plastic bags.

Maria and James watch the old loony rummaging for – what *is* he looking for? A weapon? A little keen-edged hatchet perhaps, to lop off their ears?

They huddle, cornered, barely able to watch.

Soup. Tomato. Cream of.

It's what he finds. Having located it, he delves into deep pockets, these kind of canvas bags sewn onto the outside of his greatcoat. Like a bad magician, he wallops out a tin-opener, really old.

'I'm old-fashioned,' he declares, baring his blackened teeth. 'I'm old-fashioned.' So's the tin-opener.

But he hacks off the top of the tin can while his wide-eyed audience stare, transfixed. All the time he cackles, slurps. From nowhere he produces a little saucepan – his magic's maybe getting better. An old lemonade bottle is dragged out from one of those bottomless pockets. The ancient magician opens it, pouring half its contents into the saucepan, placing the pan on the gas ring.

'What's he doing?' James whispers.

'I don't know. He's making some soup.'

'What for?'

'I'm old-fashioned,' he splutters, laughing at the tin can that's now standing in the rapidly warming water. 'I'm old-fashioned.'

'He's old-fashioned,' James whispers.

'Will you let us go, please?' Maria speaks out to the old man. 'Will you?'

He laughs himself into another cough, pointing to the can in the water.

'I think he's done that for us,' James says, uncurling himself, gazing over at the soup.

'He hasn't! Don't you dare go near him, James. He's mad, I know he is.'

'I'm old-fashioned,' the tramp nods, seriously.

'Is that your name?' James asks.

'James!' Maria hisses at him.

'It's all right,' James is trying to get up. Maria's trying to hold him down. He shrugs her away. 'No, it's all right, really.'

'James, stay here. He's mad.'

'He's Old-Fashioned,' James smiles.

Old-Fashioned explodes in to massive gusts of cackly laughter as Maria takes hold of James again.

'Get off! Let me go!'

'No! Stay here.'

'Get lost, M'ria,' James wrenches himself free again, shifting quickly across the caravan towards the warmth of the flame. 'Hello, Old-Fashioned,' he says to the old boy.

The old boy explodes, masses of hair, masses of clothing, masses of laughter.

There are lovely, tempting wisps of steam coming off the top of the water in the pan. James hunches over, warming himself. 'Maria. Come and get some of this heat.'

'I'm not going anywhere near that old nutter.'

'He's not a nutter, are you?'

Old-F, he cracks up.

'Well, he's a good old nutter, aren't you, Old-Fashioned?'

He agrees, his big beard wagging. 'I'm Old-Fashioned.'

'He's definitely Old-Fashioned,' James smiles at Maria, speaking up through Old-Fashioned's cascade of laughter.

'I don't care,' she says, 'I'm staying right where I am until I can get past him and out of that door there.'

James goes over to the door. He opens then closes it. 'You could just walk out, if you want. Old-Fashioned's not going to stop you.'

'I still don't care. I don't trust him. You don't know what you're doing, James. You don't know what he might try to do to you.'

'Come over here,' James says, cupping his hands round the flames king's-crowning round the saucepan. 'It's lovely and warm. Come and smell this soup, Maria.'

Maria tuts in disgust. The fact is, she can smell the soup from where she is. The whole place is beginning to smell of delicious cream of tomato. The crown of blue flames is tugging her to it. She tries to hold out, but cannot sit shivering any longer, watching James soaking up all the heat.

She sidles the long way round, keeping as much distance as she can between her and the tramp. Then she's by her brother's side, cupping the king's crown, her snout in the steam wafting from the water warming the soup.

Old-Fashioned laughs at a couple of blankets he drags out from under something or the other, holding them out to Maria and James. 'I'm Old-Fashioned.'

James takes one and wraps it round his shoulders.

'You must be joking,' Maria says. 'I wouldn't touch that if my - '

'Thanks, Old-Fashioned,' James says, taking the other blanket. He holds onto it.

Maria, wearing a short padded jacket, shudders.

'Is this your dinner, Old-Fashioned?' James asks, pointing to the soup in the now bubbling-hot water.

Old-Fashioned looks at it with with an expression of massive confusion and concentration on his face. He points to it, suddenly exploding into gushes of laughter. With that, he wanders away into the far corner, cosying himself on a bed of cardboard and ragged blankets.

'You see,' James says to Maria, 'it's for us. He's done it for us.'

'Well, he hasn't done it for me,' Maria insists. 'I wouldn't touch it if I was dying of starvation.'

'I am,' James says, reaching to take hold of the tin-lid that's still attached, sticking up from the side of the can. He holds it with the corner of his spare blanket. 'Do you think it'll be hot enough now, Old-Fashioned?'

The old man laughs. 'I'm Old-Fashioned.' Then he goes serious, concentrating with that confused look back on his face. Then he laughs again, his beard blowing.

'You're not going to!' Maria gasps, stepping away.

James lifts the can to his face.

'No – James!'

He tastes the soup. It is hot enough, just. The warmth melts all his insides. He gulps.

'Disgusting!' Maria cringes. 'You're really sickening, do you know that?'

James comes back out of the can. He has this orange-tomato moustache attached to his top lip.

'Gross! James, you - '

'I'm Old-Fashioned,' - in a furry of laughter.

'I'm old-fashioned as well,' James smiles, then laughs. 'Maria's not. She's modern, aren't you, M'ria?'

'I'm just clean!'

'You're just a snob. Here, go on, have some.'

'Gross!'

'All right,' James shrugs. 'All the more for me.' His moustachioed face disappears back into the can.

Maria watches him.

Old-Fashioned laughs, bucketfuls.

Maria is concentrating on her brother. 'Is it warm?' she asks.

His face reappears. He tongues the tomato from his top lip. 'It's lovely and hot further down. Brilliant. I love it.'

As he goes to re-immerse his face, Maria stops him. 'I might – I might try a little bit.'

Old-Fashioned laughs his approval.

James laughs with him, holding out the can to his sister. 'Take the blanket to hold the lid. It's hot.'

Maria brings it nearer to her face, expecting to be sickened. But the smell, the aroma from it drags her in by the nose, lapping her up and she slurps the insides of the can out.

'Hey! Greedy! Save me some!'

Maria's nose comes moist out of the can. 'There wasn't much in there.'

'You've scoffed it all. You pig!'

'Get lost, James. You had most of it.'

'You get lost, fat pig. There was loads left.'

'Well there isn't now.'

'No, there's none left, you fat pig.'

Old-Fashioned just rolls up laughing.

'What's he laughing at?' Maria asks James.

'He's Old-Fashioned.'

That appeals to the old tramp's sense of humour. He's away, rolling up.

'I'm not sure of him,' Maria says.

'He's all right,' James smiles over at him. 'Aren't you? You're all right, aren't you? See, he's good. He's - '

'Yes, I know. He's Old-Fashioned.'

They all laugh.

Some while later Maria and James are sitting round the gas ring, like some kind of camp fire. 'Do you think we should be using all his gas like this?' Maria asks.

Old-Fashioned watches them from his cardboard bed.

'No, I don't suppose we should.'

Still they sit there watching the blue flame. Old-Fashioned gazes over silently, blinking slowly every now and then.

'What are we going to do, Maria?' James asks. 'We're lost, aren't we?'

Maria stares into the ring of fire. 'A bit,' she says.

'What are we going to do? We've got to find where Uncle Peter lives. Maybe we should sleep here?'

'I'm definitely not sleeping here, that's for sure.'

'What are you going to do then, walk the streets all night trying to find your way? - No, I know, phone him. Phone Uncle Peter.'

'No.'

'No? Why not?'

'I – I've called him, I told you, from the house.'

'Yes, I know. Call him again. You've got your mobile, haven't you? You never go anywhere without your mobile.'

'That's no good.'

'Why? Why not?'

'Just – because.'

'Because? Why because?'

'Look, I don't know his number, right?'

'But you called him!'

'Yes. At home. On the house phone. His number's in that little book, the one Dad keeps.'

'So you don't know his number?'

'No! I said so, didn't I? I don't know his number, all right? Are you happy now?'

'You idiot!'

'Oh, yes? Well, why don't you make a decision for once, instead of leaving it all to me? Go on. I'm sick and tired of it, I am!'

James goes back to gazing into the flames. 'I know,' he says, suddenly, 'maybe he knows the way?'

'Who? *Him*?'

Old-Fashioned blinks.

'Yes – do you, Old-Fashioned? Do you know the way to – what's it called?'

'Breckenwood.'

'Yes. Do you, Old-Fashioned?'

Old-Fashioned laughs his beard almost off.

James shakes his head. 'He won't have heard of Breckenwood. I bet he knows every place but doesn't know the names of anywhere.'

'You're probably right,' Maria says. 'But maybe he knows the park there. Do you remember that big park?'

'Yeah. What's it called?'

'That's just what I was about to ask you.'

'It doesn't make any difference. Old-Fashioned wouldn't know it from its name, would you, Old-Fashioned?'

Old-Fashioned gets the joke, even when there isn't one. He laughs as if it's the funniest thing in the world.

'It's got that huge skateboard ramp in it,' Maria says, 'remember?'

'Yeah. Big skateboard ramp. Do a lot of skateboarding, do you, Old-Fashioned?'

He gets that one as well.

'Ray Park,' Maria remembers suddenly. 'That's what it's called, Ray Park.'

'Listen, Old-Fashioned,' James says, going over to the old fellow's cardboard bed, 'do you know it, Ray Park? Do you know the big park in – where is it again?'

'Breckenwood.'

'The big park in Breckenwood. The one with the big skateboard ramp in it? Look,' James hold out his arms in a bad attempt at miming a skateboard ramp.

'A curved thing,' Maria joins in, 'like this. Look, skateboards go on it. Ray Park.'

'Skateboards go on this curved thing,' James tries to tell him, making an arc in the air with a flattened hand, 'like this, Old-Fashioned. Ray Park, in – where is it?'

'You're as good at place names as he is. Breckenwood, for the last time. Come on. Think. Ray Park, in Breckenwood. Great big skateboard curved ramp. Like this. And a pond.'

'Breckenwood, Old-Fashioned. You must know where it is.'

But the old and puzzled tramp sits there in his origami bed, blinking. Something's going on in there, in that old-fashioned brainbox, but out here, only confusion shows.

'What do you think?' James asks Maria.

'I think we can forget it,' Maria tells him. 'Come on. Let's have a last warm before we get going. We'll find it. Eventually.'

They close in on the blue ring of flame once more, soaking in as much heat as they can before the frost - the f-f-f-f. It's out there, freezing cold and ready to cling onto them. They can see it in the twigs of the trees through the window, little needle jewels in the moon and street-lamp light.

'I can't walk for ever, M'ria.'

'No, I know.'

Neither could Maria. The heat from those flames, the warmth of the soup, it all reminds them of a greater comfort, of being asleep. It feels, at least to Maria, as if maybe she is asleep. This place, the things they're doing, all they have done, it all seems so much like a dream.

But then, 'I'm Old-Fashioned!'

Then a coughing-fit of laughter and he's up, old Old-Fashioned, lurching over to turn off the gas, throwing open the door of the caravan. The cold rushes in from outside. Maria and James are both so surprised at just how warm it has become in there.

Together, they falter on the threshold. It is hard to leave the security of four walls now, a simple floor and roof. On a night like tonight, it doesn't seem to matter how grimy the walls are, even to Maria. It suddenly feels almost like home.

But Old-Fashioned is off, striding away in his hobnail boots across the yard, his big bulk all hair and overcoat in the frost-glistening moonlight. The white light from the sky glints on the old boy's bald patch now showing quite clearly, as if it too has just frosted over.

James steps out, his training shoes crunching. 'My nose hurts in the cold.'

'That's because there's a horrible dew-drop on the end of it,' Maria has to tell him. 'Oh, don't do that! Haven't you got a handkerchief? That's disgusting!'

'Get lost, M'ria.'

'You're really revolting, do you know that?'

'Look, he's right over there. Come on.'

'Do you really think he's remembered the way?'

'I don't know. Do you?'

'I think he's old-fashioned in the head. You know, out of it. He could be taking us anywhere.'

'That's where we are already,' James says.

There's no arguing with that, so Maria doesn't, for once. She follows the sound of Old-Fashioned's boots across the yard, through the line of trees and back out to the banks of the canal. Struggling to keep up with him, Maria begins to think him a whole lot stronger than she had first estimated. When he'd come at them in the caravan, she had had the glimpse of an idea, the fancy that she could have pushed him over. Now she's glad she hadn't tried it. From the rate at which he steam-rollers forward, she's sure it wouldn't have worked.

He certainly seems to know where he's going, though. The streets ring with the sound of his frozen soles. His greatcoat and multi-mufflers show how adept he is at surviving these nights in a bed of nothing but old cardboard and cellophane.

Look how late it is now. The streets through which they wend are deserted. Even the drunks and the gangsters are somewhere sleeping like sour babies. The wendy streets echo to the ring of the frost-bitten old tramp's boots.

Maria and James follow on behind, too cold and too tired to talk much. It's all down to Old-Fashioned now.

He wanders into a graveyard, a huge and gloomy place. But Old-Fashioned marches between the tilted gravestones just as if there are no such thing as ghosts, zombies and vampires. Both Maria and James think such things exist only in stories, and that none of the stories are true. But behind each slab of gravestone there's a hideous shadow hardened in moonlight, a self-contained pit of anti-light containing all the horrors in which neither Maria nor James believe. The deep shadows loom behind them, prickling at the backs of their necks. The walking distance between them closes up as they pass beneath the overhang of a huge, frost-sparkly yew tree.

Suddenly, silently, a great white tomb-haunter lifts directly above them, sailing just an arm's length over their heads.

Maria stifles a shriek as the ghost glides soundlessly just this far, *this far* above them. James ducks. He and Maria clutch at one another.

Even Old-Fashioned stops to watch the owl sail out of sight between the forest of yew, poplar and stone-slab. He laughs. He takes a look at the sister and brother as they huddle there on the path, scared witless by a bird.

He laughs again, before striding onwards at his brisk, relentless pace.

You can die walking. James thinks so, anyway. He's going to die of it, any minute, if they don't hurry up and get there. 'Have we got much further to go, Old-Fashioned?' he asks.

The old man slows his pace for a few step, wrinkling his face still further. He glances back the way they've come. Then, the laugh. It's always there, that laugh, ready to be used to express just about anything.

'I'm Old-Fashioned.'

James and Maria both laugh with him. 'I'm old-fashioned, too,' James says.

'I'm modern,' Maria joins in, 'but I like old fashioned things.'

They're all laughing. Dog-tired, sick of walking, sore, frozen f-f-f-frost-bitten, they laugh all the more when a sign appears through the mist.

'Look, James, look – Breckenwood, it says. Breckenwood, two miles.'

'Two miles? - That's *miles*!'

But before two miles is up, they come to a park, one where a big curved skateboard ramp looms large out of the dark, heavy and frost-lit. It's way over there, and Old-Fashioned hasn't taken them there until he has taken them right there. He crunches over the grass to the ramp, stands laughing, grinning and laughing and shuffling by it as if he's about to have his photograph taken.

'You've done it,' Maria laughs, 'you've shown us the way. Thank you.'

'Nice one, Old-Fashioned,' says James, holding up his thumbs.

'Old-Fashioned,' Maria says, 'come back over here with us, please. Come and see this.'

She guides him back to the park's edge, under the sign. Ray Park, the sign says. Maria positions Old-Fashioned in front of it.

'This is where we wanted to get to. This is it. We know where we're going from here. Thank you.'

'Yeah,' says James, 'thanks, Old-Fashioned.'

The old man looks wildly confused at the sign. He glances at Maria, at James, looks back at the sign then bursts into laughter.

James laughs. Then nearly cries.

'I'm Old-Fashioned,' he says, his old-fashioned face falling, going dead serious.

'We know you are,' Maria tells him. She holds out her hand. 'I don't know how to thank you enough.'

Old-Fashioned blinks at the hand extended to him. His face folds into screwed paper without text. The out-held hand holds, suspended there in the air as Old-Fashioned gazes at it. Then, his own hand stirs, making its long way out of halfway down one of those deep, deep pockets. His old, black-fingered hand appears, gently taking hold of Maria's.

'You're Old-Fashioned,' she whispers to him.

He frowns, screwed into a ball.

Maria lets go of his hand, which remains, holding the cold air.

James steps up and clasps the hand, shaking it.

The old man laughs. 'I'm Old-Fashioned.'

'Come on, James,' Maria says. 'We have to go.'

She is walking away. James and Old-Fashioned are shaking hands as if they're never going to stop.

'We'll find you again,' James tells him. 'We'll bring you something, okay? Okay, Old-Fashioned?'

The tramp stands there, as if stunned, while James goes off after his sister, glancing back, glancing back. Old-Fashioned is standing under the sign. Ray Park, the sign says. Old-Fashioned says nothing. His hand has disappeared into his pocket again. James glances back at the sign. Ray Park, Old-Fashioned. James waves. The sign still says more than Old-Fashioned does. James wipes his eyes, runs to catch up with his sister.

When he glances back, the sign stands alone at the end of the road, too far away now to say anything at all.

Seven

Uncle Peter

They knock on the door. It's impossible to tell if the bell is working or not if you cannot hear it. So, no sound, no response, there's only the door knocker. It resounds inside the house with an empty kind of near-echo that suggests there's no one home, doorbell or no doorbell.

Maria and James both bend into the letterbox, one eye each peering into the hollow hall.

'Maybe he's asleep. Knock again, M'ria.'

The rapping sounds hopeless, and homeless.

'Shout through the letterbox.'

'Are you stupid, James? Do you really want to wake all the neighbours? Sometimes, you're just so, so – '

'Don't start on me, M'ria,' James tells her, coming away from Uncle Peter's front door. 'Please don't do it to me.'

He's too tired to suffer his sister, but she's too tired to make him suffer. They stand waiting. They are at their destination, and not there yet, both at the same time.

A postman moves from house to house along the other side of the road.

'That's the postman,' James says.

'Oh, really?'

'It must be morning. It's not light.'

'Because it's winter. If it was summer, it'd be light by now.'

'What time is it?'

'I don't know. I don't think this watch is still working.'

'Well, what time does it say?'

'I don't know. I can't be bothered to look.'

James huddles in the doorway of Uncle Peter's big empty house. Uncle Peter has no wife, no kids. He can go anywhere. He can come home when he likes.

'I wish it was summer now,' James says, blowing on his hands.

'Where is he?' Maria stamps. 'Where on earth could he be?'

'I bet he's gone away,' James says.

Maria doesn't answer.

'On holiday,' he continues.

Maria stays silent, standing with her arms wrapped round her shoulders in the corner of the porch.

'On holiday in Spain,' James says, 'where it's hot.'

Maria, definitely not hot, cannot bring herself to think about it.

'And's not coming back for two weeks. Two weeks we're going to have to standing here in the freezing cold. Two whole weeks without anything to eat or drink and no sleep or - '

'All right James! I get the message. Shut up, will you? Shut up and let me think.'

'What? All I said was - '

'I know what you said. No, don't say anything else. Don't say another word.'

'Can if I want to,' James mumbles. 'Can say what I like. Nothing to do with you. Always telling me what to do!'

'All right, then. All right! What should we do? You tell me. Go on. You tell me what we ought to do next.'

'What *can* we do? There's nothing *to* do.'

'Well, we can't stay here, that's for sure.'

'Why not? Where you going?'

'Back to the park.'

'Wait. Hang on. I can't walk any more. I'm sick of walking. I hate walking!'

'We can't be seen hanging about outside the house. If somebody notices us they'll call the police. Let's go back to the park, wait there, try again later.'

'Maybe Old-Fashioned will be there?' James suggests, but all the while knowing that this would not be so. Old-Fashioned is a real tramp. Tramps would have better things to do than stick around in some freezing park, waiting for a white winter dawn.

Maria and James don't have anything else to do, though. They can only kick around under the slope of the skateboard ramp, too cold to stop still, too tired to keep it up for long.

Some cars are going by now. Another postman pedals along on his red bike It's still as dark as ever, but one or two people can be seen walking up the road towards the station. A man unleashes his dog at the edge of the park. The dog runs directly for the big ramp. James calls and clicks his fingers.

'Don't!' Maria tries to warn him, too late.

'He's all right,' James smiles, stroking the dog's head. 'He's friendly, aren't you, boy?'

'That's not what I meant. Look now, that man's coming over. Get rid of the dog.'

'Go on, boy, run off. Go on. He won't go.'

'It doesn't make any difference now. He's coming. Don't say anything, that's all. Let me do the talking.'

So they pat and stroke the dog until the man joins them. As he approaches, he speak to his dog. 'What do you think you're doing over here, Fred?'

'Hi-ya, Fred,' James ruffles the dog's ears.

'He'll be your friend for life, he will, won't you, Fred?' He looks from James to Maria. 'Bit early, aren't you?'

'Yes,' Maria smiles, 'a bit. We like it. The frost, and that.'

'Oh, yes,' sighs the man, looking about, taking great deep breaths, 'yes, it's beautiful. Best time of the day.'

'That's what we always say,' Maria says.

'So do I,' he smiles back at her. 'Unusual though, for youngsters like you.'

'We're old-fashioned,' says James, as quick as can be.

Maria slips a smile at him.

The man laughs. 'So am I, young man, so am I. Well, nice talking to you. Must get on, Freddie needs his exercise, don't you, Fred? Cheerio. Enjoy the dawn.'

They watch the man walk away, with Freddie running back and forth, his too-big ears flapping and flopping.

Maria and James do try to enjoy the dawn, as dawn it soon is, as tired and hungry as they are. The rising sun is just beginning to illuminate all the slabs of darkness the failing moon has left behind. The traffic is moving now, with more people up and about.

'That's it,' James suddenly decides, 'it's light enough. Let's go back to Uncle Peter's house.'

'Not yet. We've got to wait - '

'I'm not waiting any more! I can't wait any more and you can't make me.'

'James! Come back! We have to wait until everyone's gone to work – James! Come back here!'

'I'm too cold. And you can't make me. You're not my mum!'

'Neither is your mum.'

'Get lost, M'ria. I wish I'd never come with you. You're too stupid. You don't know what you're doing. You got us lost and everything - '

'That wasn't my fault.'

'I don't feel well. Something's the matter with me. I just want to find Dad, that's all. Leave me alone.'

He's shrugging her hand off his shoulder. Tears are in his eyes. They feel frozen, like icy prickles distorting his vision. He's so hungry he feels sick.

Maria feels it too. She feels sick because she doesn't know what they're going to do if Uncle Peter doesn't turn up soon. They'll have to give themselves up to the police, she supposes. Then the authorities will have to put them in some kind of home or hostel, for the time being. Even separating them. Maria's heart aches to think about it.

'Look,' James interrupts her thoughts, 'there's car in the drive. Is that his car?'

'I don't know. It must be, surely. Thank goodness.'

But there's still no response to the doorbell. Nothing stirs in the house when they knock.

'Please be in,' James is praying, 'please, please.'

But nothing happens. James starts crashing away with the knocker. 'Be in! Be in! Be in!' Crash! Crash! Crash!

Maria's given up. Either he's in, or they disturb the peace of the whole neighbourhood. One or the other. She too has a go at that knocker.

Crash! Crash! Crash! Crash! Crash! Cra -

The knocker disappears from Maria's hand as the door is thrown open. Suddenly he's there, in silk dressing gown, his face a disc of crimson anger as he wonders who on earth would want to knock the wood out of the front of his house like this. He bursts out at them. He glares.

Maria and James step back. They're startled by the redness of his anger, by the fierceness of his sudden face.

But his face quickly changes. He looks as startled as they. His mouth drops open.

'It's us,' Maria says, feeling stupid.

'You – what are you - '

'Hello, Uncle Peter,' James finds his voice again.

Uncle Peter looks over their heads, peering up and down the street. 'Are you – where's your father?'

'That's why we're here,' Maria tells him. 'Peter, we're freezing cold. We've come such a long way.'

'Oh, my – what's the matter with me? Come in, come in. James, come here, give me a hug. You are cold, aren't you. I'm sorry. Come in. Go through. Let me make you some tea. Would you like some tea? Look, I'll put the heating on. The radiators – oh, that's all right, they're already warm. Here, come here and warm yourselves. Let me put the kettle on. I – you gave me such a start. I wondered who could be bashing on my door like that this early in the morning. Now, feeling better? The kettle will boil soon. Are you hungry?'

'Starving!'

'I'll do some tea and toast, shall I? Before I do, tell me, why are you here? Where's your father?'

'Well,' Maria says, taking a deep breath.

She fills him in on what has happened. She tells him their father has gone missing. Overnight, just disappeared.

He looks shocked as he makes them all tea.

Maria goes over some of the other details. Father, missing. Mrs Pearce. The police. The shoes, all still there, in a line at the bottom of the wardrobe. Her suspicions that something sinister has happened. All this.

Uncle Peter listens, almost without question. He prepares food for them as Maria speaks. He nods frequently, thinking things through.

Maria gives him more of the details. But not everything. She leaves the friction with Sandra out of it as much as possible. She doesn't bother mentioning school, or Grant. But she does tell Peter how she sneaked back into the house last night to look for clues. And how she didn't really know what she was looking for, but then how strange she thought it was that her father's shoes, every pair, had been left behind like that.

'Don't you think that's weird?' she asks him. 'That he should run away in the middle of the night, taking some clothes with him, but wearing his slippers?'

'I think it's weird that he should run away at all'

'So do I. But in just his slippers?'

'If he was overwrought, in the middle of the night - '

'Then why take anything at all? Why pack some other clothes? It doesn't make any - '

But she is cut off mid-stream. Uncle Peter suddenly dashes by to catch James.

James, with a piece of toast in his mouth, has dropped off to sleep and is about to fall from his chair to the floor. Uncle Peter prevents his fall, catching him half way down.

'That was a close one,' he smiles.

Maria manages to smile back. 'I feel like that myself.'

'I can imagine. Let me just lay him down in the other room for a few minutes, while we finish our chat. Then we can get you both to bed.'

'What about you?'

'Me? What about me?'

'Well, you've been up all night yourself, haven't you?'

He stops on his way out of the door and turns, with James sleeping in his arms. 'How do you know that?' His face has lost any signs of amusement. He looks too serious, too suddenly.

'I – we've been knocking on your door, earlier. When it was still dark. Your car wasn't out there.'

'Oh, yes. I had a date. You know.' And his smiles comes back.

Maria smiles too.

'Anyway,' he says, returning, having laid James out under a coat on the settee, 'we're all here safe now.'

'Thank goodness for that,' sighs Maria.

'Yes. Thank goodness for that. Now, about what you were telling me, about the shoes – him disappearing in his slippers like that.'

'It is strange, isn't it? You do think something might have happened to him, don't you?'

'Yes. Yes, I do. I know him. He wouldn't just run off like that, in shoes or slippers.'

Maria sighs with relief. 'Oh – I can't tell you – you don't know what it's been like.'

'No. It must have been terrible for you. With the responsibility of young James there as well. I admire you. You must be very tough. Very tenacious.'

'Tenacious, yes – if you really mean stubborn.'

'I really mean brave.'

'So what can we do?'

'All we can do at the moment is get some sleep. We're none of us much use as we are, are we?'

'No. You're right. I've got such a headache. We are going to do something about it though, Uncle Peter, aren't we?'

'Yes. Absolutely. We are going to do something.'

'Should we involve the police?'

'The police? Did you tell them about your idea about the slippers?'

'No. You know what the police are like. They don't want to get involved in things like this.'

Uncle Peter laughs. 'No, I don't actually know what the police are like. But I can imagine. As soon as they saw that message on the computer screen – that was probably enough to convince them that he'd run away of his own volition, yes?'

'Yes. It convinced me too, for a while. Until I discovered the shoes.'

'And well done for that. Now, don't worry about anything. I'm here to help. We will find your father. After we've slept, we'll formulate a plan. How's that sound?'

It sounds pretty good to Maria. Her head's thumping as if there's some massive insect in there buzzing to get out. She borrows a spare toothbrush from Uncle Peter to help wash away the bad flavour of the night, then it's bed.

It feels as though Maria's been up all her life. Bed seems like a luxury to which she has only just been introduced. The curtains are closed on the cold of the melting morning, the sheets clean and smooth, the pillow a paradise of soft, with warmth building, seeping into her joints. An ocean of relaxation floats her away to safety at long last.

Then beaches her with a crunch. There's something like a swoosh of shingle as Maria shifts through the clean sheets. A bad dream, or perhaps a feeling from outside her sleep has reached in and dragged her out of her slumber. She shudders against the mattress in a shimmer of prickly sweat. Her heart is beating wildly, banging away with her erratic breath.

Maria notices the square of curtained window is darkening. The night is coming on again. She has already slept the day gone. But that doesn't matter – it gets dark early this time of year. Perhaps she could sleep through the whole of the next night too, waking early in another morning to another breakfast, before beginning the search that will definitely return her father to her. She aches, absolutely hurts to see him. For all the tension between them, the unspoken disapprovals, the angry scenes of misunderstanding and frustration, for all that, he is still her father. He has stood by her. He is probably in trouble, perhaps in great danger.

But they will find him. Maria can allow herself to feel better about it, now that Uncle Peter is with them. At least now she's not alone, with the extra responsibility of having to drag James through it all. Yes, she can sleep, sound in the knowledge that -

Can she though? What is it that so turns her in the bed, denying her a comfortable position? The inside of her still-tired head is a mass of confused thought, images flying at her out of – out of memory? Old-Fashioned looms out of the dark frost – I'm Old-Fashioned! The leader of the gang of street-boys leaps up, barks like a dog, vanishes. Sandra's mum tuts, while Sandra whispers to someone, turning to giggle, to stare. Grant appears, begging Maria to look for clues. Uncle Peter looks surprised, shocked to see them at his front door. Have you told the police about the slippers? He asks. The desperate farewell message from Maria's father is back on the laptop screen. Uncle Peter asks again, Have you told the police?

Something seems to smack Maria in the face.

Wait a minute!

Just, wait a minute.

She has leapt fully awake, sitting up in bed, coiled as tight as a piano-wire. The smack in the face still smarts. There's something she -

What is it? What was she thinking of just then?

She was thinking of Grant. Grant, telling her to look out for clues. She was thinking of the police. She was thinking of Uncle Peter. But what, exactly? What was making her feel like this?

Something Uncle Peter had been saying to her – that was it. Was it? Was it – did you tell the police about your idea about the slippers? Was that it?

What else? Yes – this. As soon as the police saw that message on the computer screen …

The deepening square of window before her seems to darken much more, much more quickly. The gloom gathers like crystals, like black blank frost, clinging, just as icy, but with far deeper penetration. Shivers run the length, and the breadth, of Maria's spine.

Try to remember. She has to remember. Had she mentioned to Uncle Peter about the message on the laptop? Had she told him about it?

Cold shivers, icy sweat the length and the breadth of -

Had she? James, she knows for sure, said nothing about it. James had said nothing about anything really, except Old-Fashioned. She had done nearly all the talking. She had told Peter what had happened. But she had missed bits out.

Cold, cruel shivers. The crystal dark.

She had forgotten to tell Uncle Peter about the message on the PC screen. And yet he knew. He knew!

How could he know?

She had not – she's sure she hadn't mentioned it. What does it mean? What could it possibly -

The telephone sounds out. It is an alarming noise, waking up the whole house with questions, questions like – How could he possibly know?

But the telephone is not left for long. It is soon answered. Maria can hear some muffled words from downstairs. She has to hear.

So she creeps out of bed, cold in her underclothes. She wants to go to the loo quite badly. But that will have to wait.

She opens the bedroom door, slowly, as quietly as she can. The door handle gives a squeaking click. She stops. The voice downstairs has stopped. There's a maddening silence.

Then the voice comes again, speaking in the level tones of the calm. Maria slides open the door and slips out onto the landing. She approaches the staircase. Uncle Peter is standing directly below her. If the floor was to suddenly disappear, she'd land straight on his head. He is listening again, saying nothing. Maria leans over the bannister, her head tilted, straining to hear.

'It doesn't matter,' he is saying into the mouthpiece, 'you've got plenty of food, what are you worried about? You'll be all right. - No. No, it doesn't. - Anyway, listen, there's been a development.'

Maria leans further over.

'This is good. You'll like this. Listen. I've got his kids.'

Maria checks her breathing by holding her hand over across her mouth.

'What do you mean, what kids? *His* kids of course, who else's?'

Maria's eyes are screwed up, her hand clasping harder against her lips.

'They turned up here, this morning. - No, no one saw them, the police know nothing. It's brilliant, absolutely brilliant. I've got them here, in bed, like a couple of babies. He'll do anything we say now, anything. Because if he doesn't, even if he's as tough as you reckon, he won't like it when his brats are being hurt, will he?'

Maria steps away from the bannister. She is shaking. He won't like it when his brats are being hurt, that man has said. That so-called Uncle Peter.

Well, his brats *are* being hurt. They are hurt everywhere, every way they turn. Everyone close to them seems to be able to hurt them. They are already hurt, and now they are afraid.

Maria is afraid. She slips back into the bedroom, stands trying to decide what to do. While she's standing there, she hears the telephone receiver being replaced. She hears his – Uncle Peter's – footsteps on the stairs.

She leaps back into bed, hiding under blankets, her face to the wall. The bedroom door has been left too far ajar. Will he notice? If he does, will he guess that Maria's just heard that part of his terrible conversation?

The landing light snaps on. Some of the light penetrates the bedroom through the ajar opening of the door. Maria closes her eyes tighter against it. Even though her eyes are shut, she can see the bedroom getting lighter as the door is opened. He is coming in. He is standing over her bed, watching her. He, who will hurt her in front of her father to get what he wants, whatever it is. Maria can feel the hurt of him over her. She can hear his determined breathing, the strength of the lungs in a man's body she couldn't possibly fight.

But then she hears and feels him step away. The darkness returns fully as her door is closed behind him. It's not until she exhales does Maria realise she had stopped breathing entirely. She listens through her own heart beating for the sound of his footsteps going back downstairs.

As soon Maria hears a far door closing behind him, she's up out of bed again, hurriedly dressing. She's nervous, all fingers and thumbs, all thumbs and thumbs, but she is very quiet. She barely makes a sound, but to herself she is a great clumping, thumping oaf. She can still hear her own breath coming and going in stops and starts.

Then she has to negotiate that door handle again. The squeak it lets out sets all her teeth on edge. She slides out of the room, halting for a few moments on the landing to listen. Nothing.

Maria still doesn't know quite what to do. She cannot breathe properly. She feels sick. She thinks about Grant – if only he were with her. He'd know what to do. He wouldn't panic.

But Grant isn't here. And Maria mustn't panic. For James's sake, and for her own, she must keep a level head.

In James's room, there he is, still fast asleep, still supremely happy in his ignorance. Maria envies him, not wanting to spoil it by waking him. But, as before, or even more than before, she cannot afford to leave him behind.

Here goes. This is a nightmare, James. Welcome.

And she slips her hands over his mouth.

He wakes quite calmly, as if he has grown used to his sister doing things like this to him.

'Shsh. Don't say anything. Don 't make any noise at all. Will you keep quiet if I let you go?'

James gives as much of a nod as the firm handclasp will allow.

Maria carefully peels her fingers from his mouth one at a time, testing him. He gazes up at her through the gloom.

'James,' she hisses, 'listen. Don't ask any questions. We have to get away, now.'

'But - '

'No. Listen. It's Uncle Peter. He's taken Dad away. No, listen I said. Don't say anything. I overheard him talking about it to somebody over the phone. Honest.'

'Why?'

'I don't know why. They want him to do something for them. I don't know. It doesn't matter now. We've got to get away, that's all. We've got to get to the police, tell them. Come on. Quiet as you can. Get dressed. Time to go.'

Maria helps him into his clothes. Her hands are shaking. His are not. He doesn't seem to be affected by the news. Maria wonder why not, but now is not the time to question him. Now is just the time to go.

'Hurry up, James.'

'This is stupid. You are as well.'

'Yes, James, whatever you say.'

'Don't believe you!'

'Keep your voice down! What's wrong with you?'

'Nothing's wrong with me. It's you. I don't believe you any more.'

'Well I don't care if you do or not. Just do as you're told. Come on. Follow me, but keep it quiet, all right?'

He follows on behind his sister. Maria turns to check that he is with her. He pulls a face. She ignores him.

All is silent on the landing. So far so good. Maria steps onto the creaking staircase. It is old, wooden and noisy. But there is no other way.

'Come on,' Maria whispers over her shoulder. 'Quickly, down the stairs, out the door and run for it. Keep up with me.'

She steps down, one step, another. Creaking, creaking. James treads behind her. Double creaking. Every step.

Maria watches the door leading to the other rooms from the hall, expecting the mad old staircase to bring out the enemy any second. If it does, she'll make a dash for the front door, throw it open and run away screaming.

But nothing happens. They make it to the bottom. Maria reaches for the latch of the front door. They've made it. If they keep quiet enough, he'll not find out they've gone until it's too late.

Maria eases the latch and the door opens slightly. She takes a glance at James before pulling open the door.

James is looking past her, through the open doorway. Maria turns. The door is fully open, but he's there, all of him, in front of them, blocking the way. He is smiling, standing on the doorstep with his key at the ready.

He has stopped.

Maria and James stop. They stare at him, he at them, in their jackets.

He smiles more broadly. 'And where do you think you two are going?'

Eight

The Terrible Quin

'And where do you think you two are going?' he says, with the smile all over his face. 'What's going on?'

Maria looks round him, as if to assess her chances of getting past and making a break for it.

He, on noticing her glance, steps into the doorway.

Maria moves back, bumping against James.

'What's going on, Maria?'

'Oh, we just thought – we just – '

'What? What did you think?' He is stepping further into the house, closing the door behind him. 'What did you think, Maria?'

Maria forces James back up on to the lowest few stairs. 'I – we just thought we'd – go out for a bit, you know, for some air.'

'For some air? I'd have thought you'd have had enough of that last night. Going out for some air were you, James?'

James is looking, staring into the face of the man he has always called Uncle Peter.

'So, James?' his Uncle Peter is asking. 'Is that what you were doing? Going out for some air?'

'M'ria reckons - ' James starts to say.

'James!' - Maria.

Uncle Peter is glaring into Maria's face. 'Yes? Please do tell me what it is you reckon, Maria.'

'I reckon we need some air, *Uncle* Peter.'

Peter's eyebrows rise momentarily. 'Well, I don't think you do. I think you need to take yourselves back upstairs, have a bath. You must need one. I really think you ought to stay here with me, right now.'

But Maria doesn't budge. She is staring into his hard eyes. She can see it now, the truth in the coldness behind those eyes. The softness in his voice is just a lie.

'And what if we don't want to?' she asks.

'Listen,' he says softly, smiling, 'what's going on, Maria? What's all this about?'

But she will say nothing.

'James? Maybe you'll tell me. What's happening?'

'Keep quiet, James.'

'No, come on, James – tell me what's wrong.'

James takes a glance at Maria. She can see by his expression that he still does not believe there is anything bad about his old Uncle Peter.

'What's up, James?'

'Maria reckons - '

'I reckon we've - ' Maria tried to interrupt her brother.

'Let him speak for himself, Maria. James?'

'Maria reckons – she reckons you're bad. She reckons we've got to get away from you and tell the police about you.'

Uncle Peter is smiling, as kindly as he ever did. 'And what do you reckon, James?'

'I – you're Uncle Peter. That's all I reckon.'

Uncle Peter's gaze floats from James to Maria. 'Yes, I'm Uncle Peter. Nice Uncle Peter. Am I not, Maria?'

'Yes. Yes, you are. I'm sorry. I was wrong. Stupid of me. We'd better just go back upstairs and - '

'And what made you think something was wrong, Maria? Tell me that.'

'A dream. A nightmare. That was all. We'd better just - '

'Tell me – you wouldn't have been eavesdropping on my telephone conversation, would you, Maria?'

'No, I – no.'

'Are you sure, Maria?'

'Yes. Excuse me. We – come on, James.'

'No, excuse me,' he says, this Uncle Peter, reaching up the few stairs to collect James. He picks him up, hugs him, tight.

'Don't go anywhere, Maria,' he tells her. James is still as a dummy with apprehension, being squeezed too tightly in his Uncle Peter's arms. 'Don't you go anywhere, girl. Not till I'm finished with you.'

Maria has stopped. She is standing above this man, this hurtful stranger with her brother in his arms.

'You are not to move till I tell you to. Is that clear?' And he squeezes James just that little bit tighter. James has to catch his breath.

'Is that clear, Miss Maria?'

'Yes.'

The smile on Uncle Peter's face has transformed into a tight-lipped leer, his words spitting from between angry gritted teeth. 'You have obviously been listening to my private conversations. My,' - and he constricts James tighter, 'private,' - and tighter still, 'conversations. You'd better learn not to cross me, girl, or do you know what might happen to your darling little brother here? Do you? Well, let me show you, my little – Ow!'

The “Ow!” because Maria's darling little brother there has just cracked his Uncle Peter on the knee with the toe of his road-hardened training shoe. Ow! And James is tumbling out of his captor's arms onto the stairs, with that man clutching at his knee and trying to keep firm his hold at the same time.

Maria plucks James from his clutches. 'Run!' she shrieks.

They do. The only problem is, the only place they can run to is upstairs. They have to go that way, with that man limping, spitting and swearing as he chases up after them.

Into what was Maria's bedroom they dash, slamming the door behind them. Maria slides a little silver bolt into place. Immediately, he's there, crashing against the door. James is running backwards and forwards, screaming. Maria's fixed to the spot, screaming. That little bolt isn't going to take much more of this screaming, let alone the pounding that man's giving it from outside.

There's nothing in the room but a bed and a wardrobe. James dives under the bed. If there had been a chair in there, Maria would have sent it smashing through the window. She would have screamed down the whole neighbourhood until help came. As it is, she just has time to chuck a pillow at the glass before that slight bolt flies off and he's in.

He is in. He's mad, glowing, shouting. He shoves Maria back onto the bed. She is scrambling to get back up as he hauls James out by one leg. James is crawling across the carpet, trying to reach for his sister. Maria feels him grab at her arm. She snatches up his hand, tugging him to her. James is being pulled apart at arm and leg, screeching and kicking and clawing.

At that moment there comes a sharp rapping at the knocker of the front door. The madman lets go of James's leg. James crashes onto his sister on the bed.

'Help!' Maria screams.

Peter, the ex-uncle, dives falling on top of them, knocking them back and grabbing at their throats. He takes hold of them both and squeezes, squeezes. They go still, petrified. They can only just breathe. The three of them are piled on the bed, two with their throats constricted.

'Now shut up!' he wheezes down at them. 'Keep very quiet. Very, very quiet. I think you've gone and disturbed my neighbours, you two selfish brats. Don't make a sound.'

He makes them wait until another knock rattles the front door. As soon as it does, the ex-uncle is up on his feet, dragging James away by the neck.

James's eyes are nearly bulging out of his head.

'Don't hurt him,' Maria coughs, clearing her own bruised throat. 'Don't hurt him!'

'I may have to,' he tells her, with all the venom and vileness of what he is apparent now in his white, wrenched face. 'I may have to if you don't do as you're told. Or if your old man doesn't do as he is told. Do you get it?'

His whole hand is round James's throat as he holds him. James can be heard struggling for a full breath of air even from where Maria lies on the bed.

'I get it.'

'Good. Now follow me. Do exactly as you are told.'

There's another rap on the knocker as they descend the stair, James in the arms of his ex-uncle, Maria following on behind. At the bottom of the stairs, Peter the ghoul positions James behind the front door, his left hand still tightly constricting the boy's reddened throat. Maria is forced to stand still on the stairs. With his right hand, the kidnapper opens the door of his house.

'Oh, hello, Mrs Welland. I expect you're wondering what all that racket was about a few minutes ago?'

'It sounded terrible. Like a child screaming and the house being knocked down. What's going on? Is anything wrong?'

Maria is peering round the body of the man holding her brother by the throat. James, his face covered in tears, stands stiff with fear and lack of oxygen. His bulging eyes are fixed on his sister.

'No, no. Nothing's wrong. Sorry if we've disturbed you, Mrs Welland. Only I have my niece and nephew staying with me for a couple of days. We were playing a rather rough game. I expect I got them a little too carried away. I'm sorry.'

But the woman at the door doesn't seem to be satisfied with this. She's craning to see inside, to see for herself that the man next door is not in fact a monster.

The man is smiling back at his neighbour like a reptile. Slimily, he allows the door to fall back far enough to reveal his so-called niece standing safe on the stairs. Not, however, so far as to reveal the where-and-whatabouts of his strangling left hand.

'Here she is, my niece. Maria, explain to Mrs Welland here how we were playing that mad chasing game.'

Mrs Welland's face floats at the half-opened door. 'Are you all right, dear?'

Maria glances at her wide-eyed brother, at the snake-smile of the strangler, before returning to Mrs Welland. 'We're fine,' she says, with her face set an hard.

'You see,' slithers the X-rated uncle, 'all present and correct, Mrs Welland. Good to know you're keeping a proper neighbourhood watch though. Well done.'

'Well,' Mrs Welland nods, 'if everything's okay?'

'It is, rest assured. Maria, say goodbye to Mrs Welland, won't you?'

'Goodbye, Mrs Welland.'

'Goodbye, dear.'

'And a very good night to you, Mrs Welland,' his smile slips into grin as he closes the door on the retreating woman's face.

With the door shut, he lets go of James's throat, grabbing him by the scruff of the neck instead.

All James's sobs come flooding out.

Maria jumps down the stairs.

But the kidnapper lifts James clear, swinging him away, out of his sister's clutches.

'Not so fast – and you can shut up too, you little – you kicked me in the leg!'

'Leave him!' Maria demands.

'Oh! Oh, leave him, is it? Oh, I'm sorry, little boy, I didn't mean to crack the toe of your boot with my knee.' With that, he shakes James, still hoisting him by the scruff. 'If you ever do that to me again, boy - '

Maria moves forward, shoving the madman in the chest. She tears her brother from his grasp, huddling with him on the bottom stair.

James is breathless with sobbing.

Uncle Peter comes at them, reddened and ugly, his arms hanging apishly, his near-to-violence hands cupped.

Maria and James hang their heads.

He looms over them, blocking out the light.

They cringe under his dreadful shadow.

But nothing happens.

They wait. They are expecting something, another holler, a hurt. But nothing. On and on. It's horrible, this waiting, the gruesome anticipation.

Eventually, Maria has to look up. James's face lifts with hers. They see the horror-man smiling, nodding, doing an impression of his old, kind self.

'My dear children,' he smiles too sweetly, 'come, come. What did you think your old Uncle Peter was going to do to you? Eh? Stop your crying now, James. Come on, that's enough.'

Maria pats James on the back to help him catch his breath. 'Come on, James,' she whispers.

'Yes, come on, James,' Peter sways over them, 'you're okay. What did you think I was going to do to you both, you silly things?'

With that, he reaches out and ruffles James's hair. Maria shoves his hand away.

'Did you think I was going to tear your ears off, or pluck out your eyes? Did you? Darlings? - Well, let me tell you, I will if I have to. Do you hear what I'm saying? I'll hurt you so bad – you hear me, Maria? Hear me, girl?'

'We hear you.'

'You listen good, girl, because the decisions are all yours. Don't you try to get away from me again, because you won't make it. Not both of you, anyway. You'll never, ever be able to get that boy away from me, get it? You try to escape, he gets hurt. And I mean *hurt*!'

His ruddy red face is staring, *this* close to Maria's. She is holding James's head down, trying to clasp his ears closed, away from all the threats. But she can feel James hearing every word by the way he shudders, forcing himself harder against her.

This time, Maria cannot out-stare the man. She has to look away to breathe, not to be destroyed by his manic, violent eyes.

'I hope you have been listening to me, Maria. Have you been listening to me?'

She nods. Then she leaps as he shouts.

'Have you?'

'Yes!'

'Yes, what?'

She looks back at him. 'Yes I have been listening.'

'You mean,' he says, smiling again, 'yes, I have been listening, Uncle Peter – don't you?'

'Yes.'

'Say it.'

'Yes. I have been listening.'

'Uncle Peter.'

Maria pauses. 'You never were my uncle.' She's looking up at him again.

That sick, slow smile creeps back across his face. 'That's right. But now I am. I've just told my wonderful next door neighbour. I'm your Uncle Peter. What am I, Maria?' - with his face thrusting back into hers.

'My Uncle Peter,' she whispers, shakily.

'Yes!' he hisses like a viper. 'That's better!' And he withdraws his offensive face. 'Now shut that boy up, before I do.'

'It's all right, James.'

'Yes, it's all right, James.'

'No it's not,' he shudders. 'It's not all right. You've got my dad and - '

'That's enough, James,' - from Maria.

'Why do you want him?' - from wet-faced James.

He laughs, that man. 'Questions? Be very careful with your questions. In fact, keep very quiet until I specifically ask a question of you. Little children should be seen and not – well, I don't even like to see them, personally. Kids? Not me! Come on. Into the kitchen. Get sat down. Don't move, unless I tell you to. No – don't sit there together. Maria, let him sit there, you sit round the other side of the table. Go on!

'There, that's better. - I don't know, I've got quite a thirst on after all that sport, I don't know about you. Who's for a nice cup of tea? - I tell you what, you two just relax, don't make a move, and I'll brew a lovely cuppa, yes? Then we'll have to decide exactly what we're going to do with you. You can't stay here, that's for sure. Not now old dragon Welland next door's had a good look at you. I'm going to have to take you away, put you somewhere … safe! Yes. I've got somebody who'll take good care of you, don't you worry.'

The kettle boils and clicks off. He makes a pot of tea, smiling at his captives every now and then. He pours into three mugs and hands them out.

'Do help yourselves to milk and sugar, sweethearts. There you are. Lovely. - Oh, I know what you're thinking. You're thinking he won't get away with this, aren't you? You're thinking crime doesn't pay, and that good always triumphs over bad in the end, aren't you?

'You stupid brats! You know nothing about the world. Let me – allow me to fill you in. The bad run this world. The tough, the greedy, the violent, they're the ones who get things done. Oh yes, crime does pay. It pays very handsomely. Don't you fall for the lie. Crime and criminals are everywhere, and doing very nicely, thank you very much.

'Why do you think your old man and I went out of business? Bad luck, do you think? Bad business acumen? Don't make me laugh! Your father's the reason we went broke. I'm not doing this, I'm not doing that. That's unethical. That's your old man – hopeless! A big kid. No wonder you two haven't got a clue. Look at you. Pathetic. Wandering through the night, asking tramps to help you out. More than pathetic! None of you have any idea, do you. You deserve that old man of yours, and he deserves you.'

At last, at long last he falls silent. Maria and James stoop solemn-faced over their untouched tea at the table. Peter's stalking the kitchen tiles, accusing them, making himself red with vigour, white with venom. Heat-crazy he is, or snake-clammy. So many turbulent, fearful emotions are churning the insides of this man, so many vindictive, violent colours coursing across his chameleon, hateful surface.

'Drink your tea,' he orders them.

Instantly, simultaneously, they raise their mugs, doing exactly as they are told under his hot and cold cruel stare.

'And when you've finished your tea, you can both go to the loo. We've got a bit of a drive in front of us, and I don't want to have to stop.'

So, as soon as he is ready, Peter shuffles them both into the back seat of his car. Then he changes his mind. 'Get out,' he tells James. 'Get in the front seat, where I can keep you close to hand. That's it, put your seatbelts on. We don't want you getting damaged, do we? Not at this stage we don't, anyway, eh?'

Maria and James shrink under the implications behind that. He, Peter, laughs, enjoying what he has said and the effect it has had as if it were his best-ever joke.

'Where are you taking us?' Maria asks, soon after they set off.

'Never mind yourself about that. Let's just say there's someone I want you to meet. An extremely nice chap, I'm sure you'll get on famously.'

Judging by the way he is laughing, this is probably supposed to be another good joke. Maria and James just don't get it. Not that they particularly want to.

They drive away, through the dark-again streets, along a dual carriageway by a canal. At one point, Maria looks out of the window at a piece of waste ground, at the back of which sits an old decrepit caravan. The broken window she spots is dully lit from inside by what looks to be a calor-gas stove. Inside the caravan, Maria knows straight away, is an old-fahioned gentleman of the road with a riotous laugh, most probably heating up a can of tomato soup.

Maria turns away to find James peering over the back of his seat at her. She can see by the look on his face that he has noticed the caravan too. The distant look of comfort on her brother's features tells Maria that James knows the good is still out there, a warm spot in the cold night, outside the cruel atmosphere of Peter's grubby car.

Peter also notices James's expression. He looks in the rear-view mirror at Maria exchanging glances with her brother.

'What's the matter with you two?' he snaps, dispelling the moment, bringing Maria and James back to the reality of what is happening to them right now.

'Nothing,' Maria says. She can see the man examining her in the mirror.

'You two are getting on my nerves,' he says. 'I think you noticed something out there. That bothers me.'

A road sign looms by on the dual carriageway. “London 28 miles”.

'That's what's bothering me,' Peter says, nodding decisively. 'Get yourselves down, on the floor, both of you, now. Go on. Right on the floor. I don't want you looking out of the window remembering the way. Keep down. If I so much as glimpse a head between now and when we get there, there'll be trouble, understand?'

And so they have to spend the time on that long, uncomfortable journey crammed between the chairs in Maria's case, huddled into a ball in front in James's. Nobody says a word.

Maria feels sick, lying there with the tall orange street lamps gliding giddily over her, the throb and rumble of the car against her spine and the back of her head. Still she doesn't say anything. She doubts that it would be worthwhile, expecting sympathy from him. Not from him, that -

There are no words Maria can find to describe her feelings for her ex-Uncle Peter. She feels nauseous, but he sickens her more. The lights ride by over her face, but Maria feels that what's to come will be worse than this, so she keeps her silence. She watches the street lamps, the tops of tall buildings as they cross the gathering city-scape. Maria can hear more traffic, feel the uncertain stops and starts of it, see the changing red, amber and green from stop to start. Black cabs rumble next to them. Far-up windows are still lit, occasionally showing a shirt-sleeved male office-worker or smart-suited woman doing overtime at a desk.

Then, quite suddenly, all that is gone. They seem to have arrived at a different kind of place, darker, quieter, but somehow without peace. There's a massive, oppressive stillness and silence, with vast and windowless brick walls looming over them. They are driving through alleys between bland brick cliffs, all stained with age and soiled weather. There are no street lamps now, no lights from any other cars, no movement save that of their car drumming through the dismal alley-ways with its full-beam headlights ablaze.

It goes on and on. It's as if they're driving into some kind of built wilderness, a ghost town where real spectres never need a window to look out of or a door to pass through.

Rain has started to fall, black in the dark brick alleys. Maria can hear the hard juddering thump of the window-wipers changing direction over the wet screen. But she can hear more beyond that, to the cold quiet surrounding them with grim loneliness. There's no help here, no hope.

The car stops, as Maria had been expecting. The engine is shut down, the lights switched off. The no-hope silence is broken for the next few elongated seconds only by the occasional ticking of the motor beginning to cool.

'Come on, then,' the man's voice sounds deep and terrible against the new silence. 'Out you get.'

He has a powerful torch. With it, he locates James, gripping him by the shoulder. 'I've got your brother, girl. Just follow on and everything'll be okay. Come on. Watch your step.'

They are stumbling over old planks, rusty girders, crunching on broken glass. Before them, a blank, black building with even darker arches like vacant eye sockets staring way overhead. They approach the towering walls of the place, finding a tiny, broken-down door through which to enter. Inside, water's falling. It's plopping all round them into lake-like puddles on the concrete floor. There's a kind of ceiling of mesh high up above their heads.

Splashing through the lakes, they make their way across the vast floor stretched out for miles in every direction. For an instant, the torch light touches a rat. It's like a cat with a rope tail. Its eyes stab the light back at them in red laser-beams. They can hear it thudding and splashing away. Nobody says a word.

Across the other side, there's an iron open staircase. Up they go, and up they go, for an age. There's a nervous black distance under them, growing, deepening. Still they climb. Their feet ring out on the iron, echoing in the dark so far above the flooded concrete floor. Up they go, turning a corner, then up again. The ground is gone, lost way below. Maria and James cannot afford to think about it. They let it go.

Finally they step out onto an iron-grid floor, clacking their way over, sensing the mass of the air under their shoes. The panels of the floor rattle against girders. Everything is metal on this huge expanse.

But there's a light. Over there. They are heading towards it. It is showing through a window. The surprise is to find a little group of wooden huts built up here on the open metal floor. The light through the little window makes that hut look warm inside. Maria finds herself drawn towards it, almost looking forward to getting there.

As they approach the hut, their kidnapper illuminates the handle of the door with his torch. Maria and James watch his hand reach out, gripping the round brass knob. He begins to turn it. He stops.

'Oh,' he says, 'before we go in. prepare yourselves. This is the someone I wanted you to meet. If you think I'm a bit nasty, you wait till you've experienced this one.'

He turns the handle. The door opens. He shoves it, it swings in. The light gushes out to greet them.

'Let me introduce you,' Peter says, as if his mouth is beginning to water with anticipation, 'to my colleague. Let me introduce you to - The Terrible Quin.'

Nine

Andrew

First of all, there's that startling light to have to overcome. Everything is too hard and white against the ache of unaccustomed eyes. Maria and James gasp, blinking through the light to where Peter the kidnapper's colleague sits, or seems to crouch. Too pale, the bunched figure appears to be lit from inside himself somehow. There comes the sound of some kind of snake hiss, like a devil's deep breath.

Maria and James are only just inside the hut. They back away, falling against the wooden wall of the hut as the snake hiss, as the devil's breath advances. Now that they are becoming accustomed to the light, they begin to get their first proper look at the man, who isn't crouching, or sitting – The Terrible Quin.

He creatures over at them as they grimace, pressing their backs harder against the wall behind them. They want to look away, but the Quin has them transfixed, as some say serpents can do. Slimy Uncle Peter is heard laughing, a satisfied, cynical sound.

The Terrible Quin crackles, creatures, lopes. He is not squatting, but is squat, not that much taller than James, but much, much broader. His hair is startlingly white. His skin seems covered, especially on the bare forearms, in rough red lizard scales, as dry as old paper. But it is not these things that mesmerise and horrify – the Quin's eyes catch hold of a glance, hold it until it's a stare, holding it unbroken, will not let it go.

The Quin has furious red eyes.

Not bloodshot whites, but pupils as red as the rat-beads reflecting the torch light on the concrete floor downstairs. His eyes are hot, as if alight. If he ever blinks, it's as if those eyes still do not close. The red is always there, burning through.

He rustles in his scales, smiles, revealing little, hard, dry teeth, too white, pointed and perfect. His mouth is a black and white open rip across his face.

Quin rustles closer, inhumanly dry. There's a sound from his mouth, that ragged opening through which you expect to see a black forked tongue flickering. The noise he makes is the air coming in and going out of him. His inhalations sound as if they're full of metal filings. He exhales, more metallic, more filed down.

'What we gart 'ere?' an impossibly high pitched voice screeches. His red-raw gaze flickers from James to Maria, back to James.

James is flat against the wall, with his mouth fallen open, eyes half popping out.

'What we've got here, Quin,' Peter says to him, 'is a couple of interfering brats we're going to use to our best advantage, yes?'

The Quin's terrible unsmiling grin saws hacking across his crispy features.

'What have you done with our father?' Maria suddenly finds herself saying. The question spills out of her before she has the chance to weigh up the consequences of asking such a thing of this powerful little man.

The Quin terribly inhales on the shocked air. He scampers, but lizard-quick, faster than people should be able to. And he's up to Maria, hissing in her face. He's having to look up at her. She has got her face turned away slightly, but her eyes are transfixed in horror straight into the malignant red alarms of his raging pupils.

Quin looks affronted, wild with having been insulted. 'Kkshshsh!' the tongue-tied air from him warns in a hot gush. 'Don't you – don't you ever!'

That's all he says. Then he holds Maria there without touching her, pinning her to the wood with his stare. Maria cannot move, his stare is so hard and so hurtful.

'Let her go, Mister,' James's voice comes, eventually, trying to break the deadlock.

The predator's head turns with a jerk from one staring position to the next. 'Kkshshsh!' And it is James's turn to be pinned back, held fast.

Maria can feel the breath go out of her brother and the pain of panic setting in. She feels terribly pained herself, as she cannot think of anything to do to help him. There is nothing she *can* do. She is as pinned back as he is, as helpless and hopeless under the erupting-volcano eyes of the beast now holding them hostage.

Peter gives out another of his his pitiless laughs. 'I see you're pretty impressed by my colleague here. I don't blame you – Quin's pretty impressive stuff. Come on, Quin, let them get by. Get them sat down.'

But the Quin doesn't move, other than to alternate his piercing gaze between the two hostages. That rough, rusty hiss emits from him.

Then, too quickly, he moves aside. One moment he's there, pinning them down, the next he's gone, cropping up elsewhere to stand dead and dreadfully still on his thick, powerful legs.

'Move yourselves!' Peter yaps at Maria and James, pointing to a small two-seater settee in the far corner. 'Sit over there. And if you know what's good for you, you won't bother making a sound, or a move, unless you're told to. Isn't that so, Quin?'

The Quin hisses, terribly.

Maria and James are over to the sanctuary of the sofa in a second, huddled together, both reluctantly watching the grim Quin for any signs of movement. There is none. He seems not to need to breathe for minutes on end. Then there's the crude rasp of the rush of air into him, then out of him in a split second, as if the air itself doesn't like to stay inside longer than is absolutely necessary.

Who would? Maria and James wouldn't stay in the same room as him, in the same building, town, country, if they could do anything about it. But they aren't like the air – they don't get away from Quin that easily. They have to sit side by side and watch him as he and Peter effect a rasping, whispered conversation which they cannot quite hear, but know full well is about them.

Peter and Quin seem to be having a hurried disagreement about something. Maria strains to hear what they are saying as Peter's face begins to redden, as his voice elevates.

'He'll do it,' she can now hear Peter saying. 'He'll do it when we threaten his kids, so you do as you're told.'

'Kids! I don't know nothing about no - '

'You don't need to know anything! You just keep them here, Quin, you hear me? You just make sure they don't go anywhere.'

'You do it.'

'Quin, you better do a you are told!'

The Terrible Quin is seen to leap at that, to swell in every direction but upwards, flexing, puffing out like a toad. Peter can be seen to falter, backing off. The redness of his face drains to white, his lips contracting.

Quin lets out his hiss. 'Kkshshsh!'

Peter's smile comes out, but meek. His voice drops to a softened whisper, his hands spreading as he pleads with the little, frightening man.

Eventually, Quin glances over at the settee where the two are sitting in silence. He nods. Peter moves to pat him on the shoulder, but the Quin tenses, shifting away. Peter's hand veers off in another direction.

The Quin is left untouched as Peter exits, leaving the little man standing on his own. Maria and James look on, oppressed by the horrible calm that seems just one wrong word away from aggressive torment.

Quin makes his way scuttling across the room, eyes ablaze, to a little wooden chair with an open book, pages down, on its seat. He picks up the book, sits. He doesn't settle himself. He doesn't need to. The Quin just seems to stop between movements. Comfort doesn't enter into it. He closes the book, snap. His attention flits from the book to the two on the settee, snap, snap.

Maria feels James sit even closer to her.

'Matter with you two?' rustles the Quin.

Maria and James look away from him. But you can feel the Quin's eyes on you, by the concentration of heat on the surface of your skin. The place, the little dirty hut in which they're all sitting, is cold, damp – but Quin is dry, weatherproof, the heat from his eyes burning little local cringes on faces and on hands.

The Quin is violence. He is violence in the air. The atmosphere anywhere near reverberates with the hurt, the hiss and harm of him.

How long they sit there in silence, neither Maria nor James could tell. It goes on and on, that's all they know. Maria finds herself hoping that the malevolence of Quin cannot be sustained, that it will ease up, let them off a bit. But nothing gives, nothing eases, not even for a moment.

The Quin snaps open his book, thrusts his face forward into it. At any other time, with anyone else, Maria would have strained to get a look at the cover, to see what book it is. Not this time. Quin's book is Quin's book. Maria just sits sensing his concentration. She tries to listen for his pages turning, but hears none. Five or six should have turned by now, but nothing, not a movement.

The only shift, in fact, comes from beside Maria. She manages to ignore it, once. But there, it goes again.

James keeps moving, going from one position, which he holds for a minute or so, to another. Then another. Maria knows what's wrong with him. She doesn't know what to do about it, that's all.

'I want - ' James begins to whisper into Maria's ear.

The Quin starts up with a snap. His hair and scales seem to bristle and quiver. He gnashes, biting his way out of something that isn't sleep. It isn't sleep because his eyes never closed, but he seems to gnash his way back to full consciousness from somewhere deep and dangerously dark.

'Wha'?' he grinds, his shocking breath rasping. 'Wha' you say, boy?'

He has leapt so suddenly, so viciously that James has shrunk back into his collar, tongue-tied.

'He wants - ' Maria starts to speak for her brother.

But the terrible little man is on his feet. 'Don't you start to be tryin' nothin' now, y'ear me?'

'He wants to - ' Maria has another go at speaking. But the Quin's reddened face is rustling like the dead just this far from her nose. 'He wants to,' she manages to continue, looking down, speaking softly, trying her hardest not to antagonise the beast snarling in her face, 'he wants to go to the loo, Mr Quin.'

The Quin's face appears to be wiped by something at that. He backs away slightly. His white eyebrows drop, but his brow still managed to furrow. 'What you saying, girl?'

'It's just that,' Maria risks taking a look up at him, 'that we're sorry, Mr Quin, but James needs to go to the loo.'

The Quin snuffles, blinks. His breath rasps. Something in his animal mouth clicks before it closes. Then opens again. 'You better tell 'im to go outside then, you'd better 'ad. Outside.'

'Whereabouts?'

'Anywhere. It's all a' iron net. Just go.'

'But what if someone's walking underneath?'

James, listening to his sister, almost, almost smiles.

'Walkin' underneath? Well, 'ard luck them then,' Quin says, quite seriously.

James does smile. He hopes his ex-uncle Peter's taking a nice little stroll down there …

He gets up to go outside, standing quickly.

The Quin starts, backing away from the possibility of accidentally being touched. 'Stay close now,' he warns James.

'I will,' James nods. 'Don't worry.' He's not going far on that iron mesh in this dark, with rats running and dirty water and pee falling on your head.

With James outside, Maria turns to speak to Quin. 'What if I want to go?'

Quin looks over at her. 'You?'

She nods, holding his gaze.

For the first time, he looks away. 'You 'ave to do best as you can, that's all.' He picks up his book, sitting back on his little chair. 'I'm sorry,' he says, still not looking at Maria. He glances towards the door. 'Go 'urry lad along, girl. Get 'im back in 'ere.'

But as he's saying it, James is diving back in through the door, shivering.

'Get sat,' Quin yaps at him

Maria and James resume their places side by side on the settee. Maria puts her arm round James, attempting to rub some warmth into him. But the fact is, she has no real warmth to give him. The place is damp, so cold they can see their breath in the air. James's arms go round Maria's middle.

'Look!' the Quin appears from behind his book. 'What's a matter wi' you two now?'

'We're cold,' James speaks up.

The Quin stares at him. James, clasped close to his sister, returns the stare.

'We are cold,' Maria tells him.

He thinks about it, his mind churning behind the thick white eyebrows. 'Over there. Look. 'Lectric 'eater. Plug 'im in down there, see? Go on, then.'

Maria does it, pulling the wire tight to bring it as close as possible to their settee. It doesn't reach half way.

'The wire's not long enough. Can we move the seat?'

'No!'

And so they shiver, shifting, rubbing warmth into their arms. The Quin glances over at them once, twice, three times.

'Look,' he snaps, 'if you gotta do it, do it. Don't 'ave to keep askin' all the time. Do what you 'ave to. Just don't go outside without askin'.'

They get warmer. But then they get hungrier. Maria can hear James's stomach churning. Every time it does, they look at each other. They both know what's coming next.

The Quin is like a stone gnome peering into his page, always the same page.

'Mr Quin?'

'What? What the – 'oo's this Mister – what you want now, girl? What you be wantin' now?'

'Sorry. It's just that we're – we're just getting very - '

'We're hungry,' James interjects, with his belly turning over like a tumble-dryer.

'What? - What?'

'We're hungry, Mr Quin,' Maria says.

'Ungry? Forget it.'

'But - it's night time now. We haven't even had any breakfast, or anything.'

'Look, we don't 'ave nothin' for no kids' eatin'. Shut yourselves up.'

With that, he returns to his book.

James whispers, 'Maria.'

Quin looks up, hisses, goes back.

Maria nods at her brother, putting her fingers to her lips. She waits. A few minutes passes slowly before she find the courage to speak up again. 'What book are you reading, Mr Quin?'

His book snaps closed. 'Mind your own bus'ness, can't you? Eh? - Look, you want somethin' to eat, I'm gonna 'ave to go fetch it for you. I'm gonna 'ave to leave you two alone, right? You gotta promised me you don't try nothin' while I'm gone, right?'

Maria nods.

'No, girl – promise me.'

'I promise.'

'You, boy?'

'I promise.'

'Right. Just don't, that's all. There ain't nowhere you can go. There ain't no getting' away from 'ere, so don't go tryin' it, right?'

They both nod.

'Right. I shan't be long,' he's saying as he heads for the door.

'And something to drink?' Maria calls after him.

He stalls. He doesn't turn, but falters for a moment, then continues.

'Some hot chocolate,' James calls out.

The Quin halts, dead. He looks back. "Ot choclit? 'Ot choclit?' And off he goes again, shaking his head, before anybody else can call out any more tall orders.

'What they going to do to us, M'ria?' James asks, as soon as Quin has gone.

'I don't know. Nothing. Wait and see. We'll be all right.'

'So where do you reckon Dad is?'

'Here, somewhere.'

'Here, where? Where are we?'

'The old docklands, I think. These are old warehouses. There are lots of places like this here.'

'Yeah, but Dad's close isn't he? I can, like – feel him. Can't you?'

'I don't know.'

'Maria – we got to get to him. We ought to run out, find Dad. We can release him. He could get us away.'

'Could he?'

'Yeah, easy. We – let's get out, find him. He'll beat them up and - '

'Oh, yeah? He's gonna beat up the Quin, is he? Our old man, the computer expert who works out on the keyboard every day, he's going to - '

'He's not old!'

'He's too old for Quin. And what happens if the Quin gets us before we get to Dad? What do you think the Quin'll do to us, eh?'

James doesn't answer. He can't bring himself to even begin to think about it. He shudders, keeping quiet.

No one's saying anything when Quin returns with a tray of things. Now Maria shudders at the sight of him, as she still feels James shuddering by her side

'Bovril,' Quin announces. 'No 'ot choclit. Pork pie. 'Ot cross bun. Not 'ot, though. Do you?'

Maria nods. Just about anything would do them by his time. They take a mug of hot drink each, leaving Quin's on the tray. It's strong enough to almost bite lumps out of, but it is hot. Wonderfully hot. And pork pies, those little, individual ones, have never tasted so good.

As they eat, there comes another hissing sound. This one's different from Quin's usual noise. This is briefer, deeper, more hollow.

Maria and James look up at the sound of it. Quin has a little grey inhaler in his mouth. He glares at them, disapproving of the way they are staring. They look away. There's another hissing squirt before he picks up his stripy blue, steaming mug.

'Why do you want our dad?' James asks, out of nowhere.

'T'won't do you no good to be askin' questions, boy,' the Quin says, over his mug of dark fluid. 'You keep yourself to yourself now, boy, you'll be a sight better off.'

'My name's James.'

'I know,' Quin says, going back to his book.

'And mine's Maria.'

Quin grunts.

'Good book?' Maria asks, chewing on a cold hot-cross bun.

Quin's nose appears through the steam from his mug. 'Just a book,' he says.

'What is it? Can I see? Oh, Lord of the Flies. Oh, yes.'

'You know him, do you?' Quin asks.

'Who?'

'Book, like.'

'Oh, yes. We did it at school. What do you think of it?'

'Book's a book. Nothin' to it.'

'No? Oh. I thought it was pretty good.'

'That's the one,' James says, 'where all the boys are stranded on an island, isn't it?'

'Yeah,' Quin speaks softly, "spect it is. Yeah. Shut up now. You're startin' to get on me nerves.'

James looks about. The buns and the hot drinks are all gone. He sighs. 'I'm bored, I am.'

'Keep quiet, James,' Maria tells him.

'But I'm fed up. Can we play a game, Mr Quin?'

'What? - What?'

'A game. I know. I Spy. Will you play, Mr Quin?'

The Quin's terrible face contorts, puzzled. 'Play?'

'Yeah. I Spy.'

Maria is gazing at him.

He shakes his head, but slowly, speaking to Maria. 'You, like - what is it? Kids, are you? You two know who I am? Eh? You know who I am?'

'Mr Quin?' Maria suggests.

'The Terrible Quin. You know who calls me that?'

They shake their heads.

'Ev'ryone. You know *where* they first call me that? No? In nick. In prison, like. Where it be rough, I tell you – 'ard, dead 'ard. That's where they call me Terrible Quin.'

'You been in prison, have you, Mr Quin?'

'Said so, didn't I?'

'What for?'

'James!' Maria hisses.

Quin just blinks at them.

'I spy - ' James starts to say.

'Enough!' Quin shouts, starting from his chair. The book falls to the floor. 'I told you what the Quin is! Believe me, boy, I'm it! Terrible. Like, I tell you, terrible! So don't go playin' no games wi' me, boy! I'm warning you. Don't you dare show me no disrespect!'

And Terrible he is, this Quin. He is raging, red raw, flaking, rasping, threatening. Everything he says, every move he makes is a threat.

James is crushed, white. Maria can do nothing. They cower under the little man's huge outrage. He quivers in front of them, his nervy mouth twitching, his coal-glow eyes stoked, crackling.

Then he stops. He watches them, how totally appalled they are by him, how drained. He seems to falter. The rasp of his breath slows, calming. There is a hint, just a suggestion of something about him, something like regret.

'No more talkin' now,' he says. Quin takes another squirt from the inhaler as he back away. 'That's enough. It's late. You kids s'posed to be asleep by now, ain't you?'

A good while later, James is guessing what Maria's I Spy of L.O.T.F. is. 'L.O.T.F.' she repeats. 'Give up?'

'No.'

Quin's face is in the book.

Maria looks up at the stained ceiling. She is deeply bored herself, not least with having to play I Spy for what seems like hours. But mostly she's bored with being here, in this hut, waiting for something to happen. She doesn't know what the time is, but is guessing it's very late at night. They've played this stupid game for ever. Quin is ignoring them now, keeping his unwavering attention fixed into that book.

'Give up?' Maria sighs, still looking up.

But she doesn't get an answer. She looks at her brother, who has one off to sleep suddenly, slumped against the arm of the settee. 'It was *Lord of the Flies*,' she says, softly.

Now Quin looks up and over, but gently. 'Name of the book, like,' he says.

'Yes.'

He regards her for a moment or two. He has that look of uncertainty about him again. 'You - ' he begins to say, then stops himself.

Maria glances at him questioningly.

Quin looks down, then up again. 'Pretty clever, you,' he says, 'you know that, girl?'

'My name's Maria.'

'I know. I know. What you reckon, on book, like? Reckon him's any good?'

'Yes. Very good.'

Quin turns the book over and over in his hands. 'About boys, like – on some island or somethin', somewhere?'

'Yes. It's about - '

'About boys like young-un, there, eh?'

'Yes. It is a good book, but it's sort of a boys' book.'

'Oh. Ah. What book you like, then?'

'Oh, I – did you ever read *Catcher in the Rye*?'

'No, ah – no.'

'Well, that's one of my favourite books. How about you?'

'Me?'

'Your favourite book?'

'Oh. Yeah. Don't reckon I got one.'

'No?'

'Fast off, 'im,' Quin says, nodding towards James. 'Him a bit of a – bit of a nuisance, 'im, is 'e?'

'No, he's all right. He gets on my nerves. But that's just brothers and sisters.'

'Is it?'

'Don't you have any brothers or sisters?'

'Me? No. 'Ere, look, over there. Sleepin' bag. You go on 'im near the fire, an' 'e'll 'ave enough room on settee.'

'Isn't that your sleeping bag?'

'No, t'ain't. T'syours, for the now. Go fetch 'im.'

Maria goes fetch. She picks up the bag, turns to find the Quin gently laying James out on the settee. She pretends to take no notice as Quin removes James's shoes. She spreads out the sleeping bag on the floor and sits on it. Quin, as she watches him, leans forward suddenly and brushes James's fringe from his forehead. Maria cannot help but stare as the Terrible Quin quietly watches James sleeping.

Then Quin notices that he is being watched. He snaps back terribly, returning to his chair, to his nervous book. 'Get some sleep now, girl,' he mumbles.

Maria still sits there.

Quin turns and turns the book in his hands.

'I said, sleep, girl!'

'I can't sleep. How can I?'

'Boy sleeps.'

'He's a boy. He sleeps through everything. I can't do that, not any more.'

The Quin pauses, thinking. 'Nor me,' he says.

'Why are you holding my father?' Maria dares to ask.

He starts. It's almost as if he has forgotten about it, as if Maria is dragging him back to something he finds extremely unpleasant. He hisses, unable to breathe properly again.

'Don't you ask me, girl. Just - ' his breathing is rough and laboured. 'Don't – is all!'

But Maria has seen the uncertainty, the dry doubt inside him. She watches him drag on the inhaler.

'I have to - ' she starts to say.

But he snaps like an asthmatic crocodile, dry-skinned and deadly.

'Don't! Is all!'

Quin's eyes blaze, any uncertainty all burned out.

But Maria continues to watch, to gaze into the Quin. She manages to withstand the wither of his look now, now that she has seen him. That's what Maria does – she sees people. Most people, they do what they do to make others not see them, or not properly, anyway. But Maria, after a while, she sees through to them, into their secret hearts.

And she has seen the Quin. She has witnessed his dry uncertainty, this confusion from which he suffers, a personal difficulty that rasps the Quin's breath, that breaks his skin in red, scaly flakes.

'My name's Maria,' she says.

The Quin burns, rages, silently, still as stone. 'I know, girl.'

Maria looks away now, reddening, but not through fear. She turns from Quin's red, hard stare to think to herself, about him, and about herself. Just for a second.

After that second, Quin speaks again. 'Don't ask me,' he says, before he too looks away. 'Don't,' he says again, but more softly.

Maria is watching him again.

'I can't tell you about it,' he looks back at her. 'Don't you go askin' me.'

'I'm sorry,' Maria says.

The Quin gives a kind of wince, as if he's drawing his face away from a particularly nasty smell. He looks more closely at Maria. 'You, sorry? You – when we're 'oldin' your old man?'

Maria has to look down. She feels close to tears. And Maria never cries. Never. The tears are there though, prickling at the lower lids of her eyes.

'You,' Quin says, quietly, 'you – like, I dunno – kids, like. It but ain't fair really, eh?'

'No,' Maria admits, blinking, her fallen hair partially hiding her face, 'no, it isn't fair. It never is.'

'Never is,' Quin says. He's sitting forward in his chair, his raw flaking elbows on his knees, turning the book. 'You, ah – you wanna know somethink – Maria?'

Maria looks up, surprised. 'Yes.'

'I ain't never read book.'

Maria halts, pausing before she can find anything to say. 'What, never?'

'Never. Can't – seem to. Can't get them there words joined together in me 'ead makin' any sense. Don't seem to, you know, work, like. Like, I can read like, only words seem to get 'emselves all tangled, you know what I mean?'

'Yes, I understand. You're dyslexic.'

'Oh, ar? Dyslexic, is it? Most, them say the Quin's jest thick.'

Maria smiles. 'Well most of them are pretty thick themselves,' she says.

The Quin does this thing with his face. It is a smile, but this one affects the whole of his face, closing up the deep pink eyes, furrowing his brow. 'Reckon so,' he says, from within the pain of such a smile. 'Reckon you ain't far awry there.'

'Where do you come from, Mr Quin?'

'Exeter. Long time ago. Dump.'

'Really? I've been there. We quite liked it.'

'You didn't know it, girl, not like I knew. You didn't know 'oo I know, nor those same places. You know cathedral, I expect?'

'Yes.'

'Mm. Well I didn't never live in no cathedral.'

'No, neither did I.'

'No, but you lived wi' a decent bloke for a father though, that you did.'

Maria just looks her question at him.

''E ain't no criminal, ain't your dad, that's for sure. I reckon 'e be all right, tough, tougher than 'e look.'

'You haven't hurt him, have you?'

'No. But the boss - '

'Peter.'

'Ar. Peter. 'E'd 'urt 'im.'

'But you won't let him?'

'No point. I know what's gonna move some blokes, what's gonna move some others. 'Urtin' 'im don't get 'im's cooperation, like.'

'Promise me you won't hurt him, Mr Quin.'

The Quin draws away again. He examines his book, turning it over in his hands one last time before putting it to one side on the floor. He takes out his inhaler.

'Promise me, Mr Quin. You wouldn't hurt us, would you? Any of us?'

Maria can hear Quin's uncertain breath beginning to rasp. She watches him fiddling with the inhaler. 'Mr Quin? Promise you won't - '

'Shut up now, girl,' he orders her.

'But you have to promise - '

'No I don't!' he screeches. 'The Quin don't 'ave to do nothin' - '

'Yes you do!'

Quin starts up, darts up, the red eyes igniting. 'You don't – you! You don't!'

'You have to do what your boss tells you! That's what worries me, because - '

'The Quin don't!' he screams, his high voice back up to fury-pitch. 'The Quin don't 'ave to! Nothin'! You 'ear me, girl? You lissen to me - '

Maria can see how furious he is, frantic, half out of his mind. The Terrible Quin, screaming at you like that, it knocks you back, even more violently than a slap in the face. Maria's face, slapped back by the lizard approach, falls back, afraid, shocked white.

'Don't you,' the Quin hisses like a hot lizard in Maria eyes, 'don't let me 'ave to - '

But there's a sound. It stops the man in his furious, reptile tracks. The Quin clonks to a standstill, balanced on one leg, the other just lightly middle-toeing the floor.

James has stirred in his sleep.

The Quin's terrible face clockworks into the James-direction. James emits another tiny whimper. The Quin shifts slightly, his curious head tilted ever so slightly to one side.

James turns over, nestling himself into the back of the settee.

The Quin shifts again. He looks down at himself. He glances back at his vacant chair, apparently surprised to discover himself out of it. His gaze wanders back onto Maria's shocked face. He falters once more.

'Now then, girl,' he says, but more calmly, his eyes cooling rapidly, 'you just, like – no more of it. You 'ear me?'

They exchange expressions for a moment or two, wondering, each to each.

'Sorry,' Quin says, suddenly.

Their looks at one another last a few more moments. Quin's word, sorry, his surprise apology buzzes in the air between them.

The final moment passes. Quin clicks and shakes his head clear. He turns, taking up his position in the chair. He reaches for the grey inhaler that has fallen to the floor. It fizzes into his mouth. Quin draws deeply on its chemical.

'You don't always have to frighten everybody, you know,' Maria ventures, but nervously.

'Don't I? What do you know?'

'I know it's not necessary to frighten people all the time, that I do know.'

'Maybe it ain't, not for you.'

'Nor for you.'

'I'm the Quin, aren't I? The Terrible Quin. What do think the Quin does, girl? What do you reckon 'e's for?'

'For? You don't have to be *for* anything.'

'Oh, yeah you do. You don't know, girl. You ain't nothin' but a kid yet, you jest don't know what you're for. You gotta find out yet.'

'And where did you find the Terrible Quin?'

'You wanna know? Do you?'

'That's why I asked.'

'In clink – you know? Nick? Prison?'

'Oh.'

'Yeah. Oh. You try it, girl. No, you can't. You gotta try bein' like me, lookin' like me, soundin' like me, goin' in for what I goes in for. Then you know, you find out why the Quin 'as to be so terrible.'

'Why did you go in?'

Quin's face judders, glowering over at Maria in the sad electric light of the hut. 'I done 'im, didn't I – the old man.'

'Which old man?'

'The old man – my old man. Father, like. You know? Done 'im. Dead. I done 'im dead.'

Maria's mouth hangs open. The Quin, Quin the Terrible is a murderer. And Maria's there, sitting with him in the middle of the night, this murderer being one of the kidnappers of *her* father. And she's asking *him* why he went to prison.

A new, murderous silence hangs in the dirty atmosphere like a skein of sooty smoke.

The Quin looks down, remembering his inhaler. He gives himself another spray from it.

'You,' Maria manages to say, tentatively, 'you are asthmatic?'

Quin nods.

'That's why you've got such bad eczema as well. A friend of mine as both like you.'

The Quin smiles. Not the proper smile Maria witnessed earlier, but an ironic, bitter twisting of the mouth. 'Quin got a lot goin' for 'im,' he says. 'Eh? Quin's a right case, if ever there was one. - Well, now the Quin 'as got somethink goin'. For once in 'is 'ole life, somethink. You arksed me why we wanted your old man? Well, I'll tell you.

'Computer, ain't it. 'Im an' the boss, Peter, like, the two of them – computer stuff. Like, you know, them systems for banks and for bus'nesses - '

'Security systems.'

'Yeah. Well, Peter, the boss like, 'e's gonna get us more'n a million pound each, right out of computer. Right out of it – an' no one's ever gonna be able to find out 'oo took it. All we need's a bit of cooperation.'

'From my father?'

'Yeah. Only 'e don't do it, your 'ole dad. Like, 'e don't like it. Peter, 'e reckons your dad's easy, reckons I'll crack 'im like nut. 'E's all right, your old man. Like, tough, like. 'E ain't for 'urtin' no one, not like most of 'em, but 'e's tough.'

'But now you've got us to break him with.'

'Reckon so.'

'But what if - '

'No. Don't. No more. I should – I shouldn't 'ave told you.'

'But I - '

'Now! No more! Don't do no more, girl. I can't tell you no more. It's all there, it'll 'appen what'll 'appen, no more, no less.'

So they fall silent. *It'll 'appen what'll 'appen*. Maria reckons so it will, but that's hardly likely to help put her mind at rest. Maria mind seems to have a mind of its own at the moment, flitting wildly in all directions.

She takes another look at Quin, where he's sitting fiddling with his inhaler.

'Mr Quin?'

'Don't ask me, girl – don't.'

'Mr Quin, why did you kill your dad?'

The Quin's terrible face snaps like clockwork in her direction. For an instant, Maria thinks she is about to be subjected to the amok maniac-rush, the Quin in full flight right up to her face, threatening her with his appalling closeness. But his mechanical face softens to something more like flesh, although not like flesh altogether. The Quin's albino complexion never approaches even a near-resemblance of human vulnerability. But at least he eases slightly, loosening, breathing. He sucks, fizzing at the inhaler.

Maria breathes, relieved.

The Quin looks at her, on and on until she cannot return his stare. She looks down at her hands, glances up into his dead-set, red sunset eyes.

'You know,' he says, eventually, 'no one, but no one ain't never arksed me that, not since the trial, like. You – some kind of – what is it? I don't ever remember – some kind of like, like, gets inside of you. Like the boy there. Somethin' about – what he looks like, like. You know? No – I can't explain it – I just don't ever remember … '

He tails off there, rambling, confused, looking for the right words to express what he's feeing. He can't do it. He rambles off into nonsense. He can't think. He can't breathe properly. The two things are the same, with the Quin. Confusion constricts the little man's fierce breath, breaking flaky and raw over the surface of his skin.

Maria sees again, senses, again, the depth of his confusion. 'I can't imagine why anyone would want to kill their own father.'

'Can't you? That's because you only knew your dad, that's why. You gotta 'ave know my old – you gotta 'ave known mine.'

Quin's face sets in stone, fixes granite hard. He hates too, even harder than that granite.

'Did he hit you, Mr Quin?'

'Yeah, course. That's nothin', 'ittin' me. That ain't nothin'. It's 'ittin' 'er, that's what done the damage. The damage, I tell you. All that damage.'

'Who? Your mother?'

The Quin nods. "Er. Damaged. Right inside. Right inside!' he shakes his head.

Maria can hear him struggling to beathe.

'Some of 'em,' he goes on, 'they deserve – yes they do. Some of 'em deserve dyin'. That they – you know – deserve it … '

He tapers off again, too full to carry on. Maria, glancing at him, can see the fullness to overflowing of all the hurt and hate and spite in him. Maria's gone quiet. There is too much hurt, too much hate for her to cope with.

'So,' the Quin says suddenly, 'now you know. You 'appy now, are you?'

Maria shakes her head.

'Well, you should be. You got your dad to look after you, that's enough.'

'Yes, I suppose it is. He is impatient - '

'Impatient? - *Impatient*?'

'I know, I know. I do understand. But it's not easy. It's not easy for me.'

Quin does that quick smiling stretch of his face.

'It isn't. I can't talk to him. How can I, when he's always so - '

'Always so busy tryin' to get enough money to look after you, an' the boy there, eh?'

'I know. I do know. It doesn't make it any easier. And besides, it's all *her* fault really. It was all right, before she went away. She's to blame.'

'Your mum?'

'She's the one to blame, really. She's gone off to France, to act. She thinks she's going to be a great actor.'

'An' is she?'

'I don't know. And I don't care. How could she do it? She's spoiled everything. Everything!'

Quin thinks, while Maria stews. It's Maria's turn to look down, clenched, hating things.

'Look,' he says, to bring her back out, 'you remember when I told you people gotta be *for* somethin'? Well, some of us don't find out what we're for till it's too late. Some try to be the thing they're for – they jest gotta try – you know? No matter 'ow late it is – no matter what, they gotta try. You gotta admire 'em.'

There follows a deep silence. Maria tries to imagine her mother trying to be the thing she feels she really should have always been. There is so much hurt, too much confusion; Maria can hardly think through it all. But maybe, just maybe her mother does have something, some talent which drives her, demanding of her that she doesn't waste it. Who knows? Maria suddenly realises that she, Maria, does not know, that she cannot tell.

'Mr Quin?' she says. 'What's your other name?'

'Name's the Quin.'

'No, your first name.'

'I don't 'ave one, not no more.'

'But what name did your mother give you?'

The Quin shakes his head with such finality, Maria can tell that he doesn't like to think of it.

'Everybody's got a first name,' Maria says softly, trying not to sound too demanding. 'You know mine's Maria. His is James.'

'I know.'

'Then - '

But the Quin's head shakes with that resolute finality again. He has looked away this time. Maria begins to feel that she shouldn't go too far with this. You could always go too far with Quin, she feels, too easily. But just as she has made up her mind to drop it, a word comes out.

'Andrew,' comes that word, dropping straight from the Quin's mouth.

'Andrew?'

He nods.

'I like it. It suits you.'

'No, it don 't.'

'You know, Andrew, I do understand what it was you were saying to me. I do understand how people have to find out what they're best at, what most suits them.'

'What they're for.'

'Yes, what they're for. But I also know that lots of people never find out what they're for, not really. Because they make mistakes. They think they're for one thing, because that's how people make them think. But they're not. Do you know what I mean, Andrew?'

Andrew nods gain.

'I mean, it doesn't matter what they make us think we are, what problems we've got, we've got to find out for ourselves, haven't we, Andrew?'

'Reckon you're right, girl.'

'Even the most frightening person in the world,' Maria continues, 'isn't only that. There's more to them than that, Andrew, isn't there?'

He blinks at her, before looking away. 'It's late,' he says. 'You need some sleep.'

'I'm still not sure I can.'

'Try. Get in the sleepin' bag. I'll turn the light off. Go on. Get comf'table.'

He lopes over, watches while Maria settles. He switches off the light. Complete and instant darkness.

Maria listens to him making his way back to his little hard chair. 'But what about you?'

'I'll be all right. Don't you worry 'bout me. Get yourself your sleep now. You're gonna need it.'

Maria finishes settling. The floor is hard under her, but she might, she just might sleep.

'Goodnight, Andrew,' she says, into the darkness.

'Goodnight, girl.'

'My name's Maria,' she reminds him again.

'I know,' he says, softly. 'I know.'

Ten
Father

James can hear the wind. Something about the heavy-handed bluster of it reminds him how far up they are. Then he has to remember why they have climbed so high.

He looks around at the dirty old settee on which he has spent the night, at the dingy hut, with one bare light bulb hanging, the dead cup of Bovril, cold crumbs of greasy pie, and the Terrible Quin stiffly asleep on his hard wooden chair.

And there, right behind them, the previous day of nightmares, revelations, rats and dripping dirty water. The fear of yesterday rushes prickling all over his skin, threatening the day to come, with all its further, possibly greater dreads.

A panic to start it all off – where's Maria?

He sits bolt upright.

But it's all right; she's there on the floor fast asleep in a sleeping bag, her hair splayed out in every direction across the floor.

She won't like that, he smiles, judging by the dirt in this place. The morning light, falling soiled and sorry through the window shows the dirt much more than the false electric light had.

James blinks and shudders as the hut creaks and groans against the barging bluster of the wind. He drops one foot lightly onto the floor. He looks across at the Quin to see if the wind has awoken him. Quin is stone-white and still, as if dead. Nothing living could look like that, could it? Even a snake shows more signs of warmth, of moving blood. That, that thing propped there in the little chair, that gnome with the alabaster mask – surely nothing lived, surely nothing survived for long in there?

As carefully as he can, James creeps over his sister in her bag. He rubber-soles up to the Quin-mask, stands staring at it.

There is no hint of movement. It is too still, too near to death not to be dead. James reaches out slowly, his hand crossing the space between him and the cold death-mask. He's going to touch the cheek, just one cheek to feel the coldness of Quin's death in it.

But the wind blusters into the side of the hut, Wham! - and the animal eyes spring open, stinging red rays of malignant light beaming out at James like rat lasers, round and beady and full of harm.

Stepping back, he clumps into his sleeping sister, kicking her in the side, stumbling sideways onto the settee.

'What?' Maria's struggling in the bag. 'What?'

'Maria!'

'James! What is the *matter* with you? Are you mad?'

But James is crumbling under the too-steady gaze of the little man's red eyes.

Maria looks towards Quin, then back at James. 'It's all right, James, calm down.' She turns to Quin. 'He's still half asleep, Andrew. Never mind him.'

The Quin nods, once.

Maria gets up out of her bedding, throwing it over her brother. He hugs it, covering himself. The wind hammers at the hut, causing huge draughts of damp air to flag the leaves of Quin's unread book.

'Reckon you're all right, young-'un,' Quin says to James, 'eh, boy?'

James nods. 'Except I'm hungry,' he says.

'He's always hungry,' Maria smiles at Quin.

'Reckon that ain't so bad in a boy,' Quin almost smiles back at Maria.

James waits a few moments before asking, 'Can we have some breakfast the, do you think?'

Maria is still smiling at Quin. 'I could really do with a cup of tea, at least.'

He regards them, first one, then the other.

'Please?' Maria asks.

He shakes his head. But he isn't refusing them. 'You – kids, eh? Are you what kids're like, eh?'

'I am,' James smiles now, 'but Maria's awkward, aren't you, M'ria?'

The Quin laughs. James watches him closely, that laugh being like nothing he's ever seen. The mouth on Quin's face is open, all his sharp teeth showing like a row of capital As. But the sound – it's like the Quin's inhaler in reverse, a hollow slow hissing. It seems to hurt Quin, as if he has to go through so much pain to emit a single happy shout like this.

'Reckon Maria's got a lot to be awkward about,' Quin says, still nearly smiling, as nearly is as close as he ever gets.

'Does that mean we can have some breakfast, Andrew?' Maria asks.

He thinks about it for a few more moments. 'It's light out now. If I leave, you won't go tryin' anythin' now, will you. 'Cause if you do - '

'We won't, Andrew. You can trust us.'

Whenever Maria says anything like that, it seems to knock Andrew Quin, to disconcert and disorient him. He looks confused. 'Keep good an' quiet, then, 'cause if the boss finds out I leave you alone - '

He doesn't say what would happen if the boss did find out, but leaves the hut, taking last night's crockery with him. As he opens the door, a huge gust of wind labours to force it back closed again. Quin has the tray of things in one hand, but it doesn't prevent him from fighting with the weather. And winning.

When the door slams shut behind Quin, James turns towards Maria. 'Is his name Andrew?'

'Yes, it is.'

'How do you - '

'I just know, that's all. Don't ask me any more stupid questions, James. I'm not in the mood.'

Usually, that would have produced quite a response from James. Not this morning, though. Today the wind, the weather, the diminished energy in him, that peppery hint of a headache, it all combines with the circumstances to subdue him. It's worse than being in deep trouble at school.

'Maria,' he says, quietly, 'I'm scared.'

Turning away from her brother, Maria closes her eyes. Does he think she isn't scared? Can she really be expected to take much more of this?

She turns to answer him, but there comes a crash against the side of the hut. It is the wind blowing suddenly, violent enough to make Mara and James jump. They look towards the door. The hut is creaking in the wind. Nothing more happens. They let go of their breath.

But there comes another crash, a smash against the door. It flings wide and he is there, red-mad, flailing against the bluster of the wind. Peter has appeared, his angry veins full to bursting.

'Right!' he bellows against the wind, striding into the hut. 'Right, I've had just about enough!'

Maria and James back into the settee.

Peter looks about, every second redder, madder. 'Where the hell is Quin?'

Maria and James sit back hard against the back of the settee, tongue-tied, as he bears down on them.

'Well?' he rages. 'Where's Quin got to?'

'I'm 'ere,' Quin's voice comes from behind Peter.

'Where the!' Peter spins. 'Where the hell were you?'

'Right 'ere,' Quin says, looking up steadily into the down-looking face of his boss.

They front each other like that for a while, as if wrestling it out with their eyes. But it's a real old-time staring match that Peter is bound to lose. Nobody can win, not like this, not against the Quin.

'Right!' Peter snaps, spinning back round, looking for someone else on whom to vent his anger. 'You two!' he spits his words at them.

Maria and James cannot hide their hatred of this man, their old ex-uncle. Their eyes show it. Hatred is in the very exhalations of their breath. He is confronted by a wall of disgust.

He grins, sensing their bad feelings in the air. He reflects spite back at them, even as he smiles. 'I've had enough,' he says, in almost a whisper, like a very personal threat.

'Enough!' he declares more loudly, turning to the Quin. 'Enough of all this. It's time! This is it! Come on!'

At that, he reaches forward and grabs hold of James, hoisting him from the softness of the settee. Maria tries grabbing at one of his legs. James tries to kick out, letting loose a little shriek at the same time.

But Peter holds him, grips him close, dead close. He stops him. They all stop. Peter is beetroot, throbbing. He speaks through gritted teeth, his face this close, *this* close to James's. 'Don't you dare try to kick me again, boy.' He is speaking in a low, aspirated kind of whisper at James's cheek. 'You did that to me once before, you little – and I told you never to try it again. Right?' And he squeezes harder. 'Right?' And harder still.

James can't breathe. His eyes are popping, his mouth open and rounded, struggling for a bite of air.

'Right?' the quivering lunatic is demanding.

James manages a nod. It's all he can do.

'Please don't,' Maria says, standing helpless by their side, looking on.

'What did you say, lad?'

James nods, nods.

'He can't speak,' Maria tries to touch her brother. But the madman moves him further aside. 'You're holding him too tight. Oh, don't. Please don't.'

Peter turns to slide a spiteful grin at Maria.

James is gasping.

'Please,' Maria begs, hopelessly.

Then he lets James go, without putting him down. The suddenness of the release chokes James. Tears start to fall.

'Don't you dare cry,' Peter warns him, whispering too loudly into his ear. 'Don't you dare do that.'

'Please don't hurt him,' Maria begs.

'Shut up, girl! Keep quiet and do as you're told. If you don't, you know what's going to happen,' he says, through his teeth, giving James another token squeeze. 'Don't you?'

James stifles a cry.

'Yes,' Maria nods. 'I understand.'

'Good. Come on!' He marches towards the door with James like a wooden puppet in his arms.

'Quin, get a hold on her. We're going to do something about all this, you see if we don't.'

The Quin takes Maria by the arm, marching with her after his boss. Peter is stalking like a maniac, jerking along with a scared-rigid boy in his arms.

'What are - ' Maria tries to ask Andrew Quin.

'Keep it shut, girl,' Quin warns her, tightening his grip just above her elbow. 'Do yourself a favour.'

'But I just - '

The iron grip pushes still further into her arm until it hurts. 'I mean it, girl – keep it good an' shut!'

They all walk out into the running wind. It blunders into them, attempting to knock them back. They drive forward, out across the iron-grid floor, rattling towards the arches that open out to the grey blustering air.

But over there, Maria can see a figure in a little wooden chair similar to the one Quin has spent the night dozing in. He's a long way off, but Maria gasps to see who it strapped there, with his arms tied behind the back of the chair.

'Dad!' James cries out, once, before the vice of the crazed uncle grips him again, constricting his breath.

The Quin, feeling Maria tense, renews his own hard hold on her arm. 'Keep it close, girl,' he hisses at her. 'Keep it down, all right now.'

But Maria is nearer to her father now. She can see the gag round his face holding in place the hanky or rag stuffed into his mouth. She's beginning to shake, watching him struggling against the chords binding him. She can see the chair legs lift and fall as he fights to break free. She can see his thrashing feet, one slipper still intact, one flung off somewhere.

The wind is blowing his hair. It is tossing everyone's hair one way, wildly the next. Crazy Peter's bald patch is apparent to Maria as she follows him out across the platform to the arch near where her father has been installed.

James's pale green face appears for an instant over Peter's shoulder, then vanishes.

'So,' the ex-uncle sneers, stopping them some small distance from his ex-partner, 'here we all are, just as I promised.'

The prisoner goes from staring bug-eyed at his children, to a renewed, furious fight.

'Dad!' James cries.

Maria starts forward, only to be brought back, roughly man-handled by Quin, whose pincer grip does not loosen even slightly. He is hurting and bruising her arm, but now she cannot feel it. Maria feels only for her brother as he's shaken backwards and forwards in front of his father.

'Dad!' James is screaming. 'Dad! My dad!'

'Yes,' that crook shouts James down, shaking him ever harder, 'your dad! And what are you going to do about it, Dad?'

He holds James an arm's-length away as he approaches James's father. His face nears the bulging eyes above the gag.

'What are you going to do about it, Dad? Eh?'

They are staring, eyeball to eyeball. Suddenly the gag-mouthed head pops forward, cracking the other head above the right eye.

Pop!

Peter leaps back.

The prisoner is flailing in his prison-chair, the legs of it clumping up and down, rattling against the platform floor.

An even wilder wind is gusting. But it is not so wild as head-whipped Peter, now that he is hurt. He is blood red, dragging up James like a little floppy puppet.

James's mouth is open as if in a scream, but nothing comes out.

Maria drives forward against the drag-back of her keeper. He is like a heavy rock against her, preventing her from moving as he grips both arms from behind. She struggles, but it is hopeless.

'James!' she cries.

His mouth is popping, eyes wide or screwed, too open or as closed as is possible.

'James! Dad!'

But their dad can only wag in the wind, pushing back and falling forward, flinging about like a rag in a hurricane.

'Keep it, girl!' the Quin is warning Maria from behind. 'You don't wanna make it worse.'

But it cannot be much worse. Peter is approaching the edge with James, nearing the precipice at the blown grey archway that gives way to nothing but the wind. He is standing there peering over, being blown dangerously, hideously close.

James is also in a position to see too clearly over the edge. He is trying to scramble back away from it. His father fights to get nearer him. Neither of them can move enough to get where they want to go.

Maria is stuck too. Quin has her, so she is going nowhere.

'Now then!' Peter shouts out over the noise of the wind and over the edge of the precipice. 'Now then!' And they all hold their breath as he turns his back on the dreadful fall immediately behind him.

He smiles. 'That's better,' he slimes. 'That's very much better, isn't it, James?'

James is still peering wide eyed at the distant ground, the deserted concrete roadway far below.

Peter takes another look back over his shoulder. 'Magnificent,' he smiles, addressing himself directly to his ex-partner. 'Now then my friend,' he says, 'what are we going to do about my little proposition, now that the situation has changed like this?'

'Don't do it, Dad!' Maria calls, pulling against the metal pincer-grips fixed into her aching elbows.

Her dad glances over at her. He looks back at his son, wet-eyed in the other man's arms. He shakes his head.

'What,' Peter sneers, 'you still won't do as you're told, my good old friend?'

Again, a shake of the head is all he gets.

'He'll never do it!' Maria calls.

Peter snaps. 'Keep her quiet, Quin!'

The Quin does nothing.

'He won't!' Maria cries. 'He won't do it for you, or anyone!'

'Oh?' Peter gives a slimy smile now. 'He won't, will he not? Is that so?'

Maria is staring at him with furious hatred.

But that man seems to revel in her malevolence towards him. He smiles all the more, turning back slowly to face Maria's father. 'Well, we'll just have to see about that, won't we?'

Now he grins, standing tall with James almost stifled in his arms.

Suddenly he moves. He grabs James by the jacket only, swinging him round, throwing him out over the edge. It looks like a throw. But he still has hold of him by one hand – one hand only.

'No!' Maria has screamed before she can realise what has happened, or even that she has screamed.

James's father is going heart-attack mad in his bindings, fighting to break free, ready to do anything to battle these madmen. His head is going side to side.

The wind is driving everything crazy.

Maria is shrieking. 'No! - No!'

The Quin is nothing so far in all of this.

Peter laughs, hanging out the tearful fearful James to dry, swinging him out over that hideous unthinkable drop. 'Now then!' he's shouting over them all. 'Now then!' His shouts are so loud he halts them all again. 'Are you going to do as you are told, you - '

And while he swears so badly at James's dad, James is hung by the back of his jacket, petrified, stone stiff, spinning slowly, held out there by the fist of that hand.

'Are you going to do as you are told?' Peter is demanding. 'Or do I have to - ' And he almost, almost lets go of James, letting him fall, jolting him to a halt again.

James screams in terror.

Maria screams over him, flying forward against the backwards drag of the Quin.

Their father leaps in his seat. He forces forward so hard he falls, him and his chair. He smacks onto the clatter of the floor, falling sideways, still seated. He's left fighting to see, to be sure his son is still safe.

But James isn't safe, of course. He's being laughed over by the evil maniac half holding him out into the wind, suspending him precariously above the far distant ground.

'You'll do it!' he laughs like the maniac he is. 'You will do it!'

'No!' Maria screams.

'Yes!' he shrieks back, gleefully. 'Yes! Yes!' And he spins in the wind as if he's about to discus-throw James out into the void.

'No!' Maria screams again. All she can see is James's sickened face, his mouth fixed open in a silent "O", his eyes popping. She tears herself away from the hands holding on to her arms.

'Stay where you are girl!' the madman warns her, threatening to down her brother. 'Get back.'

Maria halts. She has to struggle to stay still, desperate as she is to grab back her brother.

'Quin!' mad Peter shouts.

The Quin is set in stone.

'Quin!'

Serpent-quick, Quin is at Maria, turning her away, shoving her down onto her fallen dad. She drops onto him, clutching at his tied upper arms.

'You!' Peter shouts at Maria's father. 'You'll do it!'

But the tied man shakes his head.

'You will do it!' Peter shakes James into another scream. 'You will do as you're told, won't you?'

Maria sees that her father has stopped shaking his head. She can see that he will have to give in.

'You will do it!' that red-raw grinning lunatic grins, now that he is winning.

Maria looks at the Quin where he stands with his eyes fixed on the white, petrified and down-dribbling mess that is James. 'Andrew,' she says. 'Andrew, you can't let this happen.'

Andrew Quin does not move, not one tiny bit.

But Peter has stopped. He is looking about, puzzled. 'Andrew? Who's this Andrew supposed to be?'

'Please, Andrew. Look at him. He's going to hurt James. He's going to hurt me, all of us – you as well.'

'Andrew?' Peter's asking, the sneer of a smile breaking out over his features. 'Andrew? What's this, Quin?'

'Don't let him hurt us, Andrew. Please. Please.'

'Well, well,' Peter sneers. He stands the stiffened puppet body of James upright on the metal flooring, clasping a hand over his mouth. 'Well, well, well. Andrew Quin, is it? She managed to get to you last night then, Quin, did she?'

'Andrew, please, help us.'

The Quin's response is still that of a stone. His old hard gaze hasn't faltered for an instant.

'Andrew! I've heard it all now. Quin, do your job, you idiot. Shut her up.'

'Please, Andrew, you don't want us harmed, I know you don't. He'll have to do something to us. Don't let him.'

'Do what you're here to do, Quin or I'll - '

'You're not here for that, Andrew, you're not.'

Peter suddenly looks away from Quin and at Maria. 'What do you know?' Then he looks back. 'Quin, do your job.'

'He thinks that's what you are, Andrew. He thinks that's *all* you are.'

'Quin, you know what you are. You're the Terrible Quin. You are the Terrible Quin.'

'You don't have to be that, Andrew. It's not too late.'

Mad Peter laughs. 'No, it's not too late for you, Quin. But it's too late for these poor fools. Come on, shut her up, man. Smack her one.'

'You see, Andrew – that's all you'll ever be to him. He makes you like that. You don't have to do it. You don't *have* to do it.'

Just then, the Quin glances at Maria before returning his stare to his boss.

Peter laughs. 'I don't believe what's happening here! You're actually listening to her, you little criminal.'

'Please, Andrew,' Maria speaks more softly, just above the blast and bluster of the wind.

'Please, Andrew,' Peter squirms, sneering. 'Andrew! Quin, you're nothing, and you know it. You're a little nasty animal out of the nick!'

'And he'll send you back there, Andrew.'

'I won't send you back there, Quin – you'll send yourself back! We both know it. For crying out loud, it's where you belong. It's where all you poor little dumb animals belong, tearing the guts out of each other. You're all nothing but scum! You're the lowest of the low! There's nothing more scummy than – Quin?'

That last word, Quin, with its question mark, denotes a remarkable change in Peter's voice. He has gone from crazy crowing to whimper, the colour of his face draining. He goes from red in the wind, whitening, freezing his features.

The Quin has taken a step forward. One step is all he has taken. But Quin's face, particularly his mouth, has changed. The lips are raised, the small pointed teeth showing porcelain white and serrated.

'Quin?' Peter pipes, his mouth falling open. 'Quin, think about it. A million pounds, Quin. Two million.'

But the Quin's terrible mouth is animal clenched, the teeth separating slightly. He moves forward, quivering in all his strength and compacted power.

'Quin? You fool. - No, listen. I'll give you more money. Listen – listen to me!' He is staring into the approaching savage face, concentrating so hard he doesn't notice how close he is to the edge until one of his feet slips and he stumbles forward. He glances round, horrified at the precipitous fall behind.

As Peter stumbles, as he glances round, James suddenly takes advantage of his altered concentration and tears himself away. He escapes the clutch of Peter's hand, dashing for the safety of his father and sister.

Maria reaches out and tugs James to her as Peter, turning even paler, holds out his hands to the terribly advancing Quin.

'Quin! Get back. Get back! I didn't – Quin, listen, listen to me. Quin! Quin, you little – Aaagh!'

And now the Quin is terribly on him, striking serpent-quick, in one instant standing on the ground, the next flying like a miracle through the air to clamp at Peter's throat.

Peter lets out a terrifying scream, spinning horribly, clutching at the devil at his throat as it gnashes at him. He thrashes wildly, Peter, out of his lost mind with fear and pain, crying out, spinning, crying louder. The Quin is a stone gargoyle clamped at him, gnawing at him, a nightmare dragging him round and round and round. Round and round they spin, crazy with fear and violent screams and the violence of revenge.

'Help me!' Peter cries out, at anyone.

The Quin gnaws at him.

'Help me!' the Quin's victim screams as a brash gust of wind bashes them one way, before sucking them staggering back.

'Someone, help me!' he roars, stumbling against the Quin and the wind and against his own terror.

'Help meeeee!'

This is his horrifying last cry as his staggering foot finally trips on the desperate edge that leads to the final cry and to silence.

His last cry is over. The massive, even more terrible silence remains, ringing, reverberating. Even the wind has dropped, to the ground perhaps, driving the two down, down hard and fast forever together onto the breaking concrete ground so far below.

The silence presses in on them, on Maria, on James. And on their father. He, of course, is still secured to his chair, a tourniquet belt-tight round his crammed-full mouth.

But nobody says anything, not even the wind. All is still.

They blink at the empty archway open to the grey sky. It's difficult to believe what they have just witnessed. But they have just seen it, so they have to believe it. It's over.

Their father breaks the silence at last, grunting through his gag and mouth-stoppers.

Maria seems to start awake, as if from some daytime nightmare.

James, beginning to unfreeze, wipes his nose on his sleeve. 'Undo his mouth, Maria. M'ria, undo Dad's mouth.'

Maria blinks down at the tied face of her father as it gazes up at her. He nods at her. She struggles with the knot at the back of his head. Eventually, it gives, and the gag slips away. Maria has to drag out all the cotton padding they'd stuffed into his mouth before he can speak.

'Oh, my kids,' he gasps. 'My wonderful kids.'

James is on top of him, hugging him.

'Maria, you were brilliant. Absolutely brilliant.'

Gazing towards the empty archway, all Maria can do is shake her head, once, then again.

'Maria, untie me. Come on, You're all right. See if you can untie my hands.'

'Poor Andrew,' Maria says, softly.

They all three gaze towards the archway.

'Maria,' her father asks her gently, 'please untie my hands, can't you?'

'Come on, Maria,' James says. 'Help. It's Dad. It's my dad.'

Maria watches James struggling with the hard knot of the ropes for a moment or two longer. Then she moves him out of her way, forcing the ties apart. The ropes start to fall away. Their father drops out of the support of his prison-chair.

With his hands finally freed, he kicks away the rest of his restraints. He scrambles up, taking hold of James, hugging him to his chest, long and hard. James hugs back, the two of them pressed so hard together you'd think they might never come apart again.

But Maria's father does eventually look up and at Maria, where she is standing apart, watching father and son. He smiles at her, blinking back a tear. 'You were magnificent, Maria. And maybe Quin did have some good in him, in the end.'

Maria looks down. She can feel a cry clutching at her throat, prickling in her eyes. And Maria never cries.

'Maria?' Her father's soft voice reaches for her. 'Maria?'

She looks up. He is holding out one arm to her, the other still keeping tight his grasp on James. Maria hesitates. The prickle and clutch of the cry wells up in her. She dashes forward, running into him, almost knocking them all over. She cries into his shoulder.

'Don't you ever – ever - ' she gags, unable to finish what she is trying to say.

'I won't,' he assures her. 'Don't you worry now, I never, ever will.'

Maria cries, long and luxuriously. It is such a relief. She cries until she feels she really wants to stop.

When she does, her father, puts James down. 'Come on,' he says, 'we have to go. We must go and tell the police everything.'

'Yes,' Maria agrees, wiping her face. 'Yes, we must.'

They brace themselves, knowing it isn't going to be easy or comfortable, finding their way out of this place. Their father has Maria on one side of him, James on the other, with his arms round their shoulders.

'I'm going to tell the police about Old-Fashioned,' James is saying, as they set off.

'Old-Fashioned?' his father asks, limping on his one-socked and one-slippered feet.

'Yeah, he's great.'

'Who is he?'

'Oh,' Maria smiles, 'we'll tell you who Old-Fashioned is.'

'And about those boys chasing us up the street,' James says.

'And about Grant,' Maria finds herself saying, before she can stop it.

'Grant?'

'Is he your boyfriend, M'ria?' James asks.

'No, Maria declares, 'he's not. Don't be silly. I hardly know him,' she says, but thinking to herself how she will now make sure she does get to know him.

'Ah,' their father glances at Maria.

'Can we find Old-Fashioned again, Dad?' James asks.

'Why, is he lost?'

'He gave us soup,' Maria tells her father. 'He did help us. A lot.'

'Then we'll have to find him, I suppose,' their father says, smiling at James. 'Now, on the way, tell me all about it. All of it.'

'We will tell you,' Maria says, 'but before we do, can I ask one question?'

'What's that?'

She hesitates. 'You wouldn't – you wouldn't ever think of marrying Sandra Pearce's mum, would you, Dad?'

He stops them. They are both looking at him, intently. He laughs. 'No way,' he says, shaking his head. 'Of course I wouldn't!'

They smile, relieved.

Maria kisses him. 'In which case,' she says, 'we'll tell you all about it.'

And they do.

First published by
Orion Children's Books
Orion House
5 Upper Saint Martin's Lane
London WC2H 9EA

26354102R00110

Made in the USA
Charleston, SC
04 February 2014